ALEX SPARROW
and the Really Big Stink

For my family: Stanley, Teddy, Mia, Helena, Luis and Dean, with all of my love.

ALEX SPARROW
and the Really **Big Stink**

by Jennifer Killick

Firefly

First published in 2017
by Firefly Press
25 Gabalfa Road, Llandaff North, Cardiff, CF14 2JJ
www.fireflypress.co.uk

A CIP catalogue record of this book is available from
the British Library.

print ISBN: 9781910080566
ebook ISBN 9781910080573

This book has been published with the support of the
Welsh Books Council.

Typeset by: Elaine Sharples
Original cover art by Heath McKenzie

Printed and bound by: Pulsio SARL

1

The World According To Me

Have you ever wanted to be a secret agent? A bad-A, undercover, villain-busting super spy, like Nick Fury, the top dog at Marvel's S.H.I.E.L.D. agency? Well, don't get your hopes up – it takes a special kind of person and years of training to get that job. I've been working on it since I was four and up until a couple of months ago being accepted into S.H.I.E.L.D still seemed a long way off. Sure, you can do a hundred star jumps a day to make you strong, and keep chasing the scabby cat from next door out of your garden to make you quick, but some spy skills are a bit harder to come by. For example, how can you tell if someone is lying? People lie all the time. Especially grown-ups – mums, dads, teachers – all of them. And I'm not just talking about the obvious lies, like pretending the battery is dead when you're stuck in a boring queue and want to play games on their iPhone, or saying you did really well at sports day when you fell on your face and came last. No, this stuff goes *way* deeper. Grown-ups tell lies that you would never guess about: not in a million years. Maybe you're thinking, 'Well neither can you, bigmouth, so shut up and go back to your push-ups'. But I actually can. You want to know how? It's classified information, Top Secret Agent Business, but if you promise to keep it to yourself, I'll tell you.

First of all, let me explain how it started. I'm Alex, by the way, Alex Sparrow. I live at home with Mum, Dad, my little sister Lauren and our boring pet goldfish. I'm ten, in Year 6 at Cherry Tree Lane School. I've never minded school, and back then, when all this began, I was cruising along nicely. I was pretty much the leader of my group of friends (all boys, no girls, obviously) and we were really popular. Everyone wanted to hang around with us and people looked up to me, you know? Life was awesome, or at least I thought so at the time, until one night, when everything changed...

It was a warm September Friday and Mum and Dad were on one of their Date Nights (it's an embarrassing, old-married-people thing). They got Donna to come over and babysit Lauren, and I had a nag-free evening to myself. I thought I'd take the opportunity to watch some hardcore PS4 gameplay clips on YouTube – the ones made by American dudes who swear all the time. My mum's well hysterical about stuff like that and legs it across the room to slam down the lid of the laptop if anyone says anything even slightly bad, like 'jeez' or 'shizzle'. *So* annoying. Anyway, I was halfway through a super-intense walkthrough when, randomly, Superman's theme song started playing and this pop-up appeared, surrounded by shooting stars and about a hundred emojis:

Alex – Who Can You Trust?

Find out with The Professor's Amazing Lie-Detector.

Only £19.99 – Accurate Results Guaranteed.

Now, I'm no idiot. I know these things are just cheap plastic rubbish, made in China. A complete rip-off. But for some reason, maybe because I was wired on Coke and Tangfastics, maybe because I'd been listening to too many American swear words, maybe because the Superman tune was making me feel like doing something daring, I had this urge to get it. I swiped Mum and Dad's emergency credit card from its not-so-secret hiding place (they really need to re-think their kid-proofing techniques), agreed to the terms and conditions and bang. It was done.

What happened next was weirder still. The second I clicked 'Send', the home phone began to ring, which pretty much never happens, because who even uses a home phone these days? When I answered it, what sounded like a recorded message clicked on. A woman's voice said: 'Thank you for your purchase from The Professor's Laboratory. Your lie detector will be with you before you know it. Good luck, Alex.' As the message clicked off, I heard a loud crackle and what felt like a spark of electricity seemed to jump from the phone to my ear. It kind of jolted inside my head, like when you touch a metal door handle in a shop and get an electric shock, but much worse. It really hurt, but just for a second. I shouted some abuse into the phone but there was nobody there, so I hung up, wishing I'd left it for Lauren.

I did think it was all a bit strange, but then I started to get a headache so bad that I actually wanted to go to bed, which *never* happens. I tucked myself in with some teacakes and a packet of ham, and fell asleep before I even had a chance to hide the wrappers under my pillow. That was the last time I went to sleep feeling like a normo; the final sleep before the start of the Really Big Stink.

2

Stuff Happened That Is Totally W-ear-ed

The next morning I went about my business as usual. Mum and Dad like a lie-in after their Date Nights, and when they finally come down, they're all kissy, which is disgusting. I made Lauren some Cheerios and did myself some toast so I could be back in my room on the PS4 before they appeared.

Next thing, Mum walked in and said to Lauren, 'Good morning, poppet, did Alex get you your breakfast?'

Lauren put on her baby face and said, 'No, Mummy, he only maked his own breakfast.'

This is the weird part. As she told this flipping outrageous lie, something happened. I heard a low, buzzy noise, and the inside of my right ear kind of vibrated. It was like my ear was farting, I swear. Mum didn't frown and Lauren didn't do her usual 'Urgh – disgustering!' so I came to the conclusion that nobody else had heard it, though I thought I could detect a faint eggy whiff. I was a bit surprised. My ear had never farted before, in fact, my earholes were the only bodily openings which never made a peep. So I did what anyone would do – stuck my finger in and had a root around. Nothing there but wax.

Mum gave me her huffy look and poured Lauren a bowl of cereal. Lauren smirked. No respectable agent would let that sort of behaviour go unpunished, but as Mum was there, I'd need to be extra-sneaky in my quest for revenge.

I walked casually up to the tank where Lauren's pet goldfish lived. I gently tapped the glass. 'Don't you think Miley looks a bit different, Mum? Sort of bigger, and oranger?' Miley – the original Miley – had died. I knew this because it was sort-of-accidentally my fault: a science experiment gone wrong. Apparently, Red Bull doesn't give goldfish wings. But nobody knew that I was responsible. I hadn't seen the point in coming clean, as I'd learnt my lesson, was a better person for it, and nothing was going to change the fact that Miley was belly-up. But the next day, Miley was swimming around in her tank, though she didn't look quite the same.

Mum shot a look at Lauren who was peering into the tank.

'Why does Miley look different, Mummy?'

'I don't think Miley looks different … she's just got a bit fat. Fish often get fatter in the winter, because they eat more to keep them warm.'

On hearing this frankly rubbish attempt at a lie, my ear trumped again – louder and with a definite pong. Just like before, nobody seemed to notice, though Mum and Lauren were very distracted by the goldfish catastrophe I was cleverly constructing.

'Really?' I asked, with my most innocent face on. 'Do they change colour in the winter, too?'

'Yes!' Mum said, in a squeaky voice. 'Goldfish are very festive. It's their version of wearing a Christmas jumper.'

Once again my ear rumbled.

'It's only September though, Mum.' I felt quite sorry for her; Lauren was squinting at Miley and Mum was starting to panic.

'This may sound crazy,' I said, 'but to me it looks like someone replaced Miley with another fish. Is that even possible?'

I looked at Mum. Lauren looked at Mum. Mum looked like she'd wandered into a nest of velociraptors.

'No. Of course not. No. No. Not at all.'

A big, bubbly fart echoed inside my ear and the smell of poo filled the air. Lauren was looking from Miley Mark 2 to Mum and back again like she really wasn't buying it. As she started screwing her face up for a full-on screaming fit, I took a brief moment to enjoy the results of my stealth-revenge-attack and then ran up to my room to think. I had a sneaky suspicion that something was up, but I needed expert assistance. I needed Google.

After fifteen minutes of thorough research on the web I had ruled out pretty much every ear-related lurgy I could think of. There was no pain or 'discharge of mucus' (yuck) which ruled out the worst ear illnesses. And there was no ear disease on the whole of the world wide web that involved a nasty stink. It was a bit freaky and, I'm not going to lie, I was scared. I even thought about calling an ambulance. Something stopped me.

My ear had farted every time someone told a lie. How was that possible? And was it just for today, or would I be able to keep doing it forever? For an agent-in-training, it was the perfect skill. It wasn't even a skill. It was almost like a power. A slightly disgusting superpower.

I thought about the origins stories for all my favourite superheroes; many of them were normal guys, living boring lives, until the day a chance meeting or unfortunate accident gave them their powers and changed everything forever.

But I was already Agent Alex Sparrow, an epic bad-A with added swag. If anyone deserved a superpower, it was me. I really had to find out what was going on.

So, that's how it started. No lie. Since then, a lot has happened. I was an idiot with it at first, swaggering around, thinking I could do anything I wanted. I had to learn the hard way that it isn't so simple. 'With great power comes great responsibility.' In my case, with a bit of power comes a lot of stink. And the trickiest thing about it all? Knowing that somebody is lying is not the same as knowing the truth.

3

What's That Smell?

I went to school on Monday with a mission. I'd had most of the weekend to think about how I could use my power and I came up with loads of good ideas, most of which involved me ending up super-rich or flying a stealth jet to Moscow. Or both – preferably both. But first I was going to test my power on the people I knew. Imagine all the delicious, juicy stuff I could find out about my friends and teachers. I walked to school chuckling and rubbing my hands together, but only in my head because actually doing it would seem mental.

The moment I walked in the gates, I realised it wasn't going to be that simple. Surrounded by hundreds of noisy, chatting kids, my ear was going off all over the place. Buzz after buzz after buzz. The trouble was, I couldn't distinguish between conversations, let alone pick out the lies. And the smell, which hadn't seemed that strong in my house – damn, it was bad. Luckily, in the middle of a crowd, it was easy to avoid being identified as the source.

I found my friends, Jason, Kyle and Ronnie, hanging out at the usual place round the back of the science garden.

'Good morning, gentlemen,' I said, in the manner of a young Tony Stark at an Avengers breakfast meeting. 'I hope you all ate your Weetabix: something tells me it's going to be an eventful day.'

'What are you on about, Sparrow?' Jason sneered at me.

'Yeah, why do you always act so strange?' Ronnie asked.

'Alex likes to talk as if he's in a comic. He thinks he's a superhero.' Jason again.

They all laughed. They laughed at me a lot, which I thought was a good thing. I'm a funny kind of guy, like Deadpool from X-Men but with less swears and violence. And now I had a power too.

Part of me wanted to tell them about it, but I knew that once I'd put it out there, I wouldn't be able to take it back. Plus, Ronnie and Kyle had really big mouths and they'd spread it round the school in no time. Maybe I'd tell Jason later when the others weren't around. He could be my sidekick!

'I don't think I'm a superhero,' I said, which made my ear fart extra fartily, making me wonder if my own lies smelled worse than other people's.

'Yeah, whatever.' Jason made a face. 'What the hell is that disgusting smell?'

Luckily the bell rang for the start of school, so I didn't have to try to answer. I didn't realise it then, but those words were going to become like the soundtrack to my life, which was disappointing because I'd sort of hoped it was going to be 'Uptown Funk'.

I used the morning PALS session to go over my plan. 'What the flip is PALS?' you're probably thinking, just like we did when they told us we'd be doing it at school. Well, PALS stands for Positive Aspirational Life Skills and basically involves a lot of talk about 'inner peace' and 'wellbeing'. The whole school had to attend a PALS session every morning after registration. They were run by the new teacher, Miss Smilie, and we had to sit in the school hall for ten minutes while they played boring music that nobody has ever heard of, ever, and put these videos up on big screens. The videos were pictures of dolphins and kids playing in the park, with words written over the top. Stuff like, 'I am a happy, healthy and productive member of the school' and 'I radiate peace and positive energy'. They're called affirmations and we're supposed to repeat them to ourselves through the day. I know, a right load of rubbish, we all thought so too.

Miss Smilie took it all really seriously and walked up and down the room like a sentinel, trying to make us concentrate. If she caught anyone messing around she'd make them report to the PALS Suite at lunch. We liked to wait until she was looking the other way and say 'bogeys' or 'bum' as loud as we dared and watch her head whip round, her red smile flickering as she tried to work out who the culprits were. She was fighting a losing battle with this PALS business, if you ask me. There was no way she could make a bunch of kids want to meditate – it was a complete waste of time.

But that Monday I was happy to sit through it because it gave my ear ten minutes to chill out. I hadn't been prepared for the mass of ear buzzing that being at school had caused: clearly everyone lies pretty much all of the time. If I was going to find out anything interesting I would have to separate people and interrogate them by themselves. It was going to be a long day.

I thought up loads of ways to speak to people one-on-one: going to the bin to throw my pencil sharpenings away whenever anyone else did, borrowing people's rulers, getting tissues, and going to the toilet, hoping for a chance meeting with someone else trying to escape maths for a few minutes... I found out many interesting things by first break. Like that Mini Minnie in Year 3 really does have a purple belt in karate and that Big Bad Bhavi in Year 5 most definitely loves Taylor Swift.

Walking around school knowing that I knew things that nobody else did made me feel pretty good about myself. I maybe, possibly, kind of started to get a bit cocky.

It was a rainy day, so at breaktime, we had to stay in for wet play. I noticed Carrie-Anne Clarke putting PALS posters up on the noticeboards and I decided she would be my next target. She was one of those especially annoying girls who told the teacher if you were messing around in the lunch line or made a joke that involved wee or poo. She wouldn't even say 'wee' or 'poo' because, according to her, it was 'inappropriate'. She'd won Star of the Week twice already, and we'd only been back at school for three weeks. It would be brilliant if she had some shocking secrets.

'Hi Carrie-Anne, I see you're putting up some posters.' It's important to act casual when you are approaching a target. If you show any sign that you are about to probe them for information, you will spook them. I leant against the wall with the confidence of a young Thor looking over the puny Frost Giant army he is about to destroy.

'Oh yes, helping hands make happy hearts.'

'Then your heart must be super-happy – you've put posters pretty much everywhere.'

'Sharing these wonderful affirmations is a gift I can give to everyone.'

So far, so loserish. Time to find out what she really thought. 'Do you really love helping, though?'

'Oh yes, of course.'

Not lying.

'Even at break when the teachers who should be doing it themselves are probably just eating cake in the staffroom?'

'Our teachers work hard to guide and nurture us. They deserve a break and our heartfelt thanks. Besides, putting up the posters gives me the perfect opportunity to re-read the affirmations.'

Still not lying.

'What about these affirmations? "The only way to be in style is to dress your face up with a smile!" Do you agree?'

'That's one of my favourites.' She beamed at me.

Unbelievably: not lying.

'But what if you're feeling sad?'

'Why would I feel sad?'

'What if someone stole your *Frozen* backpack?'

Girls love *Frozen* more than life.

'*Frozen*'s just a silly fairy story. I gave that backpack to the charity shop and got a PALS one instead.'

Actually not lying. I couldn't understand it.

Jason, Kyle and Ronnie came over and I thought I might as well give up on Carrie-Anne and do something less disappointing, like find out who stole my Pokemon card last term.

'I'm happy that you're so interested, Alex. If you like, you can help me with the rest of these posters,' Carrie-Anne said, loudly enough that everyone heard. 'As we work we can go through the affirmations and really think about what they mean. But first I'd like to offer you some advice: if you lean, you won't look keen. You should probably straighten up.'

My mates started sniggering.

'Hold on a bit, I'm not interested in putting up posters or learning affirmations.'

'Then why were you asking so many questions?'

'Yeah, Alex,' Jason said, 'why were you asking Carrie-Anne so many questions? You must really like affirmations or maybe you're in love with Carrie-Anne.'

So embarrassing. Think, Alex. 'I was asking questions because I'm making a film for my YouTube channel called "Ten Things That Suck". PALS affirmations are at number eight and annoying girls are number one.' Yeah, it was a mean thing to say and I felt bad. It was also a lie. My ear farted.

Carrie-Anne looked hurt. 'Miss Smilie is on lunch duty today. I'm going to report your inappropriate behaviour, Alex Sparrow.' She walked off.

'Since when have you had your own YouTube channel?' Jason was dying to make me look bad in front of everyone.

'For ages, since that thing all that time ago, that was ages ago. At the time of that thing.' Oh, poo.

Jason sniffed the air and wrinkled his nose. And then Miss Smilie came into the room. Perfect.

Miss Smilie was always smiling, at least her mouth was always smiling, but not her eyes, which were too open and starey, like they were painted on. And her hair always stayed exactly the same, like a Lego person's hair, even when it was raining, or windy. I reckon there could have been a hurricane and it wouldn't move. She was like a weird, shiny, plastic person. And not in a good way.

'Can anybody explain what has been going on here? I've been advised that people are disrespecting others and, if you can believe it, making fun of PALS! OMG, I thought, I must get the goss on this.' She smared at us, which, if you didn't know, is what happens when someone smiles and glares simultaneously.

'I'm not sure, exactly, Miss,' I said, 'I was just offering to help Carrie-Anne put up posters and she somehow got the impression that I was being rude. I would never be rude about PALS, or Carrie-Anne because they're both awesome.' The fartiest fart exploded in my ear and a flipping terrible smell seeped into the classroom.

Miss Smilie sniffed and took a step away from me. 'I'll accept that this was a simple misunderstanding between chums. In fact, I'll go and tell Carrie-Anne you'd like to help her with the posters. She'll be positively thrilled. And you can all run along outside now. The rain's stopped and I'm sure we could all do with some fresh air.'

She walked out of the room. Extremely quickly.

Jason was grinning in a way that made me very uncomfortable. 'I'm Alex Sparrow: I love Carrie-Anne Clarke and I turn into a scared little girl when I see Miss Smilie,' he said in a pretend girl's voice.

'Shut up, Jason.'

'Serves you right. You've been acting weird and annoying all day. Not so smug now you've just been shown up by Smilie.' He looked round at everyone else. I sensed this wasn't going to end well for me. 'To be honest, I think you must have pooed yourself, Sparrow, because you STINK!'

And then everyone started laughing – really laughing: jaw-aching, bent-over-holding-their-stomachs laughing.

Most super-agents would stand their ground: face the danger head on. But most super-agents didn't smell like a mouldy dog poo. So I did the only thing I could do. I ran away to the one place I knew I could be alone.

4

Bossy Girls and Pigeon Poo

Let me just say that I have never, ever sat on the Friendship Bench before. It's OK for the Reception kids to go there; they're small and don't know anything about life yet. But for a Year 6 kid to resort to the bench? It's like wearing a sign saying: 'Hey everyone, check me out – I'm a loser!' But I was desperate and I stank like the boys' toilets on curry Tuesdays.

I sat down on the cold, cold wood and leant forwards, trying to cover my face with my hands so no one would recognise me. What would Nick Fury do in this situation? If only I had a brilliant disguise – some glasses, a fake nose, maybe a moustache – I could conceal my identity while I found a way to get rid of my stupid ear power. I didn't know exactly how I'd got it in the first place – possibly I'd breathed in a radioactive fart, or I'd been hit on the head by a meteor – the hows and whys hadn't seemed that important when I was thinking up ways to use it for my own entertainment and great personal gain. I hadn't realised it was one of those life-ruining lie-detectors you never hear about.

'Hey, dude, you do realise you're sitting on the Friendship Bench. Are you new or something?' I looked up to find a girl from one of the other Year 6 classes standing over me. I was pretty sure her name was Jeff, but I'd never spoken to her because she was a bit weird. She was short, with messy blonde hair and blue eyes so bright that they looked like the infinity gem from Loki's staff in *Avengers Assemble*. She had the standard school uniform on but it seemed kind of different on her, although I couldn't work out why. Maybe it was because of the way she was standing, hands in pockets, her mouth doing this frowny-pouty thing, looking at me like I was the biggest moron on the planet. Her mistake, but I'd better own up.

'It's me, Alex Sparrow from 6C.'

'So you're not new?'

'What do you mean "new"? You must recognise me. I've been at this school since nursery. I'm pretty popular.'

'Maybe. You look kind of familiar.'

'I was the angry badger in the nocturnal animals assembly.'

'Don't remember it.'

'I won the best dancer award at the disco last year.'

'Didn't go.'

'I hang around with Jason Newbold.'

'Who?'

'Jason Newbold. I've got a really big group of friends.'

'Then why are you sitting on the Friendship Bench?'

'You know, just relaxing, chillaxing...'

'Well, can you do it somewhere else? I'm on bench duty, so if you sit here, I have to keep talking to you. It's getting cold, there's a weird smell and I don't want to waste my time with someone who doesn't need my help.'

So I still stink. But, more importantly, this girl has a serious attitude problem. 'Jeez, maybe you should think about chilling out. I don't exactly want to be talking to you either.'

'Then get off the bench.'

'How about you get off my case?'

'I'll get off your case when you get off the bench. There might be kids who are actually lonely and upset and not sitting here because you are. You're abusing the rules of the bench. It's selfish and wrong.'

I was about to tell Miss Bossy Mouth exactly what I thought of her bench police routine when a pigeon swooped really low, about a centimetre away from my face, and landed on the bench beside me. I hate pigeons. My mum says they carry germs and spread diseases like rats, and this one had beady eyes and a toe missing from one of its feet. I would have jumped up under normal circumstances, but there was no way I was moving from that bench. It was a matter of principle.

'Get lost, stupid dirty pigeon!' I shouted. 'Get your manky foot away from me.'

The pigeon just shot me what I could have sworn was a dirty look, if pigeons were capable of having facial expressions. Then it looked at the girl.

What happened next was weird. I'd seen a lot of weird over the past few days, but this was way-up-the-top-of-the-weirdness-scale weird. The girl started shaking and shuddering, like she was having some kind of fit. It looked kind of like she was trying to dance but had lost control of her body. Her arms and legs sort of jerked in all different directions and her face went through a series of horror expressions. The only time I'd seen anything like it was in games and films and on TV, when people get bitten by zombies. Zombies. Could she be turning into a zombie? Was I witnessing the start of the zombie apocalypse? I know I should have wanted to help her but, to be honest, I was totally freaked out. I was too young to have my insides eaten. Then I realised I could run away to call a teacher. Running away was a good option. I would look like I was helping but really I'd be getting myself to safety and looking for weapons. Win-win.

I stood and turned, ready to run, but I heard

something that made me hesitate. The girl was spitting out random words and short sentences which didn't make much sense. But then she said, 'Who is The Professor?' I froze. The Professor. I bought a lie detector from an internet pop-up sent by someone called The Professor. Could it be a coincidence?

The girl stopped twitching at the same time as the pigeon took off from the bench. We both watched in awkward silence as he flew away, circled back and dropped a massive, slimy poo on my shoulder.

'Serves you right,' the girl said. Apparently she hadn't turned into a zombie.

'Erm, firstly, what the heck just happened to you. And secondly, how, when I just risked my own personal safety to make sure you were OK, does it serve me right that some scabies-ridden pigeon pooed on me?'

'Number one, bench-boy, I had a strange experience at the weekend and it's given me a twitch. And number two, it served you right for being so rude. Dexter didn't appreciate being called manky.'

'You've named the pigeon?' The girl was crazy.

'No, I didn't name the pigeon. It's his name.'

Super crazy.

'How do you know? Was he wearing a badge?'

'Because that is the most important question to be asking right now…'

Why was she looking at me like I was the nut job? I was missing something, but what? Think Agent Alex, think. And then I realised: The Professor! How much did this strange girl know and how could I find out without giving away any of my own secrets? I had to play it cool – I had to play it like a super spy.

'Why were you yelling "who is The Professor?" just now when you were, you know, having some kind of zombie freak-out?'

'Because I want to know who The Professor is, obviously.'

'Are you referring to a specific The Professor? Professor X, maybe, or Professor Snape?'

'I was referring to The Professor who sent me an internet pop-up on Friday night.'

She must mean *my* 'The Professor'! I tried not to let the excitement show on my face. 'And what was the nature of this "pop-up"?'

'I think you can guess that I bought something from The Professor.'

I forgot about keeping my calm exterior and not giving anything away.

'Was it a lie detector?'

'No, why? Is that what you got?'

Damn.

'Well, it might have been. Or it might have been something else…'

'Right.'

'So what did you get?'

'I can communicate with animals.'

'No way!'

'Yep.'

'But that's impossible.'

'Apparently not.'

If what this rather abusive girl was saying was true, then I really did have a power, and it must have come from The Professor and his Pop-Up of Trickery. Not to mention his Recorded Message of Excruciating Pain. This was a Very Big Deal.

'You could be making this up. How do I know I can trust you?'

She raised an eyebrow again and just looked at me. What was she playing at? It was no time for games.

'Well?' I said.

She sighed. 'You got a lie detector, right?'

'Well, maybe, yes, but I don't see what that has to do with it.'

And then it hit me. Oh yeah, I could tell if someone was lying. My ear hadn't farted once during our conversation, which was, I supposed, a pretty good indication that she was telling the truth.

'Oh. Yeah. Sorry. My bad. So you have to do that freaky zombie-dance every time you talk to animals? That's hilarious!'

'It's not the best.'

'So your friends have ditched you too?'

'Because I've developed a twitch? Course not. They're my friends; they wouldn't disown me because of a twitch. That would be stupid.' Jeff, or whatever her name was, frowned. Well, frowned even more than before. 'Is that why you're here? Did your friends disown you because of your power?'

I didn't want her to think I was a loser. 'No, no, just having a time out, that's all.' The lie made an especially nasty odour.

'Right. But you have a side effect too.'

'It's not a twitch though. It's a stink.'

'That explains a lot.'

'You two must have something very exciting to talk about, if it means ignoring the bell and being late for registration. Please, do share it.'

I jumped. Miss Smilie was standing over us, her smile glued to her face. I wondered if she'd had plastic surgery to fix it like that, or had a nasty accident with some acid, like The Joker. Her eyes flicked from me to the girl and back.

'So, it's Alex, isn't it? And Jessica? What's going down with you BFFs?'

'It's Jess, actually.' (Oh, Jess!) Jess just stared at her with the most disgusted look on her face. Clearly it was up to me to talk us out of trouble.

'Sorry, Miss, we were just having a discussion about the affirmation of the day.'

'Really? And what were you discussing exactly?'

'Well, I was saying that I preferred Friday's one, the one about small ripples and leaping fish and all that, but Jess was arguing that today's is better. She's really into radiating positivity.'

I tried not to inhale the farty fragrance that was mingling with the autumn breeze.

'Are you, Jessica?' Miss Smilie said, hopefully too suspicious to notice the stink.

She snapped her face back round to Jess, who said, in the most deadpan voice, 'Yes. I'm radiating as we speak.'

There was a moment of silence as she carried on staring and smiling, first at Jess and then at me.

'I'm glad you're taking the affirmations seriously. They really can inspire you to be better people. However, being late for registration is unacceptable. If I catch you loitering again, you'll be spending your breaktime in the PALS room with me. The world won't wait for those who are late!'

Jess managed to look even more disgusted, which I wouldn't have thought possible.

'You're right, Miss,' I said, while grabbing Jess's arm and pulling her towards the main doors. 'You should hashtag that and make it tomorrow's affirmation of the day. We'll be going now.'

With one last hard stare at each of us, she walked off.

Jess turned back to me and said in a whiney sort of voice, 'Yes, Miss, sorry, Miss, we were just discussing affirmations and peace and love and joy.'

'Well, one of us had to say something, and it got rid of her, didn't it?'

'I suppose, but you could have gone with something slightly more believable.'

'What could be more believable than you radiating positivity? I've only known you five minutes and I can already tell you're like a ray of sunshine.'

I had loads of questions to ask Jess but we had to get to registration before we got in proper trouble. She obviously thought the same, because she just said, 'I'll meet you after school by the main gate,' and started stomping off down the corridor before turning back and adding, 'and look out for anything strange'.

What the fudge was she talking about? Other than the whole lie-detector business, and Darth Daver, the weird kid from 6P, who hardly talks, wears too much black, and pulls his sleeves right down over his fingers, the only strange thing I could see at school was her.

More importantly, I had my own flipping super-cool superpower. Well, not that cool. If I was summoned to some kind of superhero meeting I'd roll up and it'd be like:

'Hi, I'm Electro-Man, I can shoot lethal electric lasers out of my eyes.'

'Hey, I'm Aquaboy, I can swim faster than a shark.'

'Hello, I'm Alex, my right ear farts whenever somebody lies.'

Maybe I could get some kind of uniform. But then I don't think stretchy tights are really my thing. I tried on some skinny jeans once and I nearly couldn't get them off (there was talk of scissors – it was so embarrassing). If I couldn't change in and out of my costume at the speed of light, I'd have to wear it all the time and that would be a very bad idea. Darth Daver gets so much abuse just for coming in on mufti days with his nails painted black.

There was so much to think about – names, costumes, gadgets – that I kind of forgot about what Jess had said, and I only remembered I was supposed to be meeting her when we were packing up at the end of the day.

5

Darth Daver: My Hero

At 3:30, I went to meet Jess at the school gate. I didn't know what to expect, what with her being so strange and bossy, but at that moment she was the only kid in school who actually wanted to talk to me, even if it was just because we both bought special powers with horrific side effects from some evil genius called The Professor. Whether I liked it or not, I needed her.

Unlucky for me, when I got to the gate she was standing there talking to Darth Daver. I should have known she'd be friends with him; he's possibly the only person in school weirder than her. Even unluckier for me, Jason, Kyle and Ronnie were just behind me. If I ever wanted to get back in the gang I couldn't let them see me with her. I crouched down and tried to hide behind a group of kids. They were walking one behind the other in a really neat line, like soldiers or something. It was a bit odd and it made it hard to get in among them so nobody would see me. Good thing I'm a super-stealthy secret agent and can make myself practically invisible. I crept toward the gate, staying close to the ground, congratulating myself on my first-class sneaking skills. Until a pair of stompy black boots stepped into my path. Jess stared down at me, one eyebrow raised.

'Are you trying to hide?'

'Hide? Er, no. I was just tying my shoelace.'

I guess she didn't need to sniff the air to know that was a whopping lie. Awkward.

'Your shoes have velcro straps,' she said.

'Well your shoes are boots, which are against uniform policy, but you don't see me giving you a hard time about it.' Distraction. Nice save, Alex.

She turned to Darth Daver and said, 'This is Alex. Alex, this is…'

'Darth Daver…' I said. There was no avoiding it now. I looked around just in time to see Jason, Kyle and Ronnie laughing really hard as a conker pinged off the side of my head. Someone had thrown it, and so fast that even with my lightning reflexes I was taken by surprise and fell back, right on my butt.

'Found some freak friends that stink as much as you, Sparrow?' Jason shouted loudly so everyone could hear.

How was I supposed to answer that? I tried to think of some excuse, something to make it clear to Jason that these weird kids were not with me. But before I could speak, a scabby hand reached down and firmly but gently pulled me to my feet.

'Are you OK, Alex?' Darth Daver brushed some dust off my jacket sleeve.

'Yes. Yes, I am. Thank you Darth Daver.'

'No worries, dude. See you tomorrow.'

Darth walked out of the school gate. Jason and the others had gone too. It was just me and Jess.

She looked at me like I was a total moron. 'You know his name is just Dave, right?'

I'm ten now, so Mum lets me walk to the corner by myself and she picks me up from there. Jess is eleven, so apparently she can walk home completely on her own, *and* she has her own phone. She lives in a flat with her mum a few roads away from me. She texted her mum to say she was coming over to my house for a bit and her mum was totally chill about it, because apparently, 'they're more like best friends than mum and daughter'.

When we got to the corner, my mum was completely annoying. 'Ooh, who's your new friend? When we get home, I'll get you some snacks and then I'll leave you two alone. Lovely to meet you, Jess, hope to see you again *very* soon.' Well embarrassing.

Jess and I walked ahead so we could chat. I know Mum was thinking I wanted Jess to be my girlfriend and I didn't want Jess to get her hopes up, so I made sure there was a big gap between us and I tried to be a bit rude so she wouldn't get the wrong idea.

'So, Jessticles – you don't mind if I call you Jessticles, do you?'

'Yes. It's offensive.'

'But it really suits you! Anyway, what was that pigeon saying to you at lunch?'

'He said he works for The Professor.'

'He works for The Professor? How does he "work" for The Professor?'

'He wouldn't tell me much. He said they can't have stuff "getting out" and he has to be sure that we aren't, erm, grasses.'

'But I mean, what does he do for The Professor exactly? Carry his shopping? Put the bins out?'

'I don't know. All he said was that he works for The Professor and that there is something bad happening at our school. We were both given powers so that we can find out what's going on. He also said The Professor hopes we have our powers under control.'

'Under control? What does that mean?'

'I assume it means we can make it so that we can choose when to use them.'

'So yours goes off all the time?'

'Yeah, I can hear the voices of every animal around me, even the ones I can't see, like the birds in the trees and the mice in the undergrowth. Why are you smirking like that?'

'Undergrowth. Makes me think of hairy bottoms.'

She sighed. 'I don't need to ask if yours goes off all the time…'

So my stink was still following me around.

'Then we need to start trying to control our powers and to track down The Professor,' Jess said.

'Ooh, a mission!'

Agent Alex was back in the game.

We sat in the kitchen eating pizza and making a list of ways we could try to find out where The Professor was. First, we got to work on the web. Have you ever Googled 'The Professor'? If you want to learn a lot of stuff about some woman from Victorian times who wrote books with her sisters, give it a go. If you want to learn the whereabouts of a mysterious scientist who tricked you into paying £19.99 for a life-ruining lie detector, don't bother. We spent ages going through page after page of rubbish and couldn't find a single lead. You'd think that if other people had been innocent victims of this nutter's telephone electrocution, there would be some evidence – posts, blogs, something – on the web. But there was nothing.

We trawled through the phoney professors, some basketball player, some DJ, some mental old guy from New York who apparently walks the streets throwing popcorn at people. None of them looked scientisty. None of them could be our The Professor.

I had plenty of other ideas, but Jess thought most of them were stupid.

'Match.com.'

'Pardon?'

'Match.com.'

'Er, why?'

'Think about it. Being a professor must be a lonely job. All those long, cold nights at the lab. He's probably desperate for a Mrs Professor to go home to.'

'Maybe he already has a Mrs Professor. The recorded message on the phone was a woman's voice.'

'She sounded too young to be Mrs Professor.'

'Why? The Professor might be young.'

'Jess, you idiot. Everyone knows that all professors are old with glasses and crazy white hair.'

'You're the idiot, Alex. Why don't you come up with some ideas that don't completely suck?'

'At least I'm coming up with ideas.'

While we were working, I could feel someone watching me. I looked around but there was nobody there. Nobody but Miley the goldfish swimming around her tank and peering at me with her bulgy eyes.

'Jess, would you please tell Miley to stop staring at me all the time? It's really off-putting.'

'Fine, though she's probably only staring because you have a freakishly oversized head.'

'I do not! Do I?'

Jess was at the fish tank, twitching away. I thought it would be a short conversation. What could a dumb goldfish possibly have to say? But there was a lot of talk going on. Jess asked the odd question, but mostly there was just silent twitching.

'Well?'

'His name isn't Miley, it's Bob.'

'That's a weird name for a girl fish.'

'He isn't a girl, dufus.'

'Oh. Is he really stupid?'

'No. He's amazing. Very perceptive. And because he observes all day every day, he knows loads of stuff.'

'No way, and there was me thinking he was brain-dead.'

'Alex, we've been through this before. He can hear you!'

'Oh yeah, my bad. Sorry, Bob.'

'You're lucky he can't poo on you.'

'If he's so smart, why does he just swim in circles all day?'

'What do you expect him to do? Write an essay? Perform brain surgery?'

'Well obviously not, the paper would get all soggy and he doesn't have the appropriate tools. But he could do something cool, like back flips or blowing bubbles in the shape of different exotic fruits. Ask him why he swims in circles. Go on, ask him!'

Jess asked the question and I waited impatiently while she spasmed through his really long reply.

'He has to swim in circles. He can't stop. He has a routine.'

'Come again?'

'He has a routine – swim seven circuits clockwise, then seven circuits anti-clockwise. He can't break the routine, it's very important to him.'

'What if he wants to chill?'

'He doesn't chill, unless it's scheduled. He needs to keep everything in order or he gets upset.'

'Blimey. Someone needs to learn how to relax.'

'Not everyone's like you, Alex. Thank God.'

'But that's mental! Proper OCD!'

'Again: He. Can. Hear. You.'

'Oh yeah, soz. Each to their own and all that.'

'He wants me to pass on a message to you.'

'What is it?'

'He says you eat too much ham.'

6

The Only Way To Be In Style Is To Block Your Ear Stink With A Rubbish Hat

After our research on The Professor turned out to be a total waste of time, I'd spent the rest of the evening trying to control my power so I could show off to Jess. I tried the obvious things: putting scrunched-up toilet paper in my ears and poking around with a Lego lightsaber. The toilet paper just made everything sound muffled and I poked too far with the lightsaber and made blood come out of my ear. I hate blood, especially when it's mine. In the end I found an old hat of Dad's with earflaps attached. It looked completely stupid but I thought it might keep some of the smell in.

The next morning I sat down for registration hoping that the rest of my class had somehow been victims of a random group accident which had wiped their memories. Maybe something involving a giant bear with rabies. That would be cool. No such luck.

'Hey, Alex! I hope you had a bath last night. And this morning. Stinking weirdo.'

I didn't need to look round to know it was Jason's voice. People started sniggering.

'Hey, Poo-Breath! Did you get that hat off a tramp?'

More laughing. I'm not usually one to ignore that kind of abuse but I couldn't think of anything to say that wouldn't make things worse. I carried on writing rude names for Jason on the desk with my finger and thinking about how Batman didn't have to put up with this kind of treatment.

I felt something hit my arm and the laughing increased. Then something else struck the back of my neck. The laughter got louder as more people joined in. I turned my head and found that my sweatshirt was covered in gluestick-coated missiles. There were bits of rubber and balled-up paper stuck all over me. Mum was going to kill me when I got home.

I picked a paper clip off my sleeve. 'Ooh, I need some new stationery. Thanks, Jason, you've saved me a trip to WH Smith.'

'I thought I could decorate your tramp-hat.' Jason was really enjoying himself.

'Most of it landed on my back, so you have a rubbish aim. Probably why you can't get on the school cricket team.'

While Jason sat fuming and trying to think of a witty comeback, our teacher, Miss Fortress, walked in. Miss Fortress always looked tired and annoyed. It was like her trademark look. Yoda had his cool hooded robe, Nick Fury had his eye patch, and Miss Fortress had her 'up-all-night-drinking-coffee-and-worrying-about-stuff' face – you never saw her without it.

'Good morning, Miss Fortress,' we all chanted.

'It is morning, I suppose, but whether it's good or not is another matter.'

'Miss Fortress,' Jason said, 'Alex has been messing around with the gluesticks.'

My ear vibrated and a particularly horse-manurey smell swirled through my nostrils. It was like being at a farm.

'Miss Fortress,' Jason called out, 'can I move seats? It really stinks around here.'

'Jason, it's only 9am and you're already giving me a headache. Just go to PALS, all of you, so I can have ten minutes without anyone getting on my nerves.' Miss Fortress was never at her best in the morning.

'But Miss Fortress,' Carrie-Anne raised her hand, 'you haven't taken the register.'

'I'll just make it up. Nobody checks things like that anyway. Off you go.'

We all filed down the corridor to PALS, where I made sure I sat right at the back. That way if anyone threw anything at me, I'd be able to see it coming.

It also gave me the perfect viewpoint to check out what was going on. Most of it was same-old, same-old – the usual yawns, fidgeting, and notes being passed when Smilie wasn't looking. But something was different. Some of the kids were acting strangely. They were sitting up, watching, listening and paying attention. Let's be clear, there were always a few kids who did that in PALS. The Carrie-Anne types who always got the most merits, the best parts in the school shows, brought in cards for the teacher that they'd made themselves at home. You know the ones I mean. This wasn't the same: these kids were riveted. They were watching the PALS screen like it was the best movie they'd ever seen. They didn't look away for a moment, or slouch, or scuff their feet on the floor. Their hands were clasped in front of them, all *neatly*. And the weirdest thing was that some of these kids were the baddest kids in school, the ones who were always in trouble. Or they had been.

When I met Jess at lunch, I was excited to tell her about what I'd seen. I spotted her talking to Darth Daver so I had a quick look around to make sure none of my mates were about to see me with them, and then I went over.

'Hi Jess, hi Darth Daver.'

Darth Daver looked up and smiled. 'Hi, Alex, nice hat!'

I thought for a moment he was being sarcastic

but then realised my ear hadn't gone off, so he must have actually meant it. It was the first nice thing anyone had said to me for days.

'Hey, thanks, Darth Daver.'

'You do look marginally less One Direction than usual.' Jess said.

We all chatted for a while and I had to admit that it was nice to have people to talk to. When I was with my old mates, my ear went off all the time but it didn't fart once with Jess and Darth. Maybe my power had gone away, or maybe I had it under control. Or maybe they just didn't lie. When Darth Daver went to band practice, I got my chance to talk to Jess about our investigation.

'I think I might have some intel on our mission.'

Jess raised an eyebrow. 'Intel? Who do you think you are, James Bond?'

'Duh, no, I'm much younger, handsomer and spyier than him.'

'Right. What have you found out?'

'Some of the kids are acting strangely. They're being really good.'

'You interrupted my conversation with Dave for that? Wow, my mind is blown.'

Jess's inappropriate sarcasm made my ear go off, so clearly my power hadn't gone away. I was disappointed but, more importantly, I was very mad with Jess.

'Firstly, I don't see what's so bad about me joining you and Darth Daver. You were probably just discussing what song you want played at your funeral or something like that. At least when I'm around you talk about things that aren't depressing. I'm like a hashtag-smiley-face. I did you a favour. And secondly, the kids are being weird-good, not normal-good.'

'Like how?'

'You want an example? No problemo. You know that Year 1 kid who pushes everybody, the one we call Pushatron 2000?'

'Everyone knows him, though not everyone calls him by such a stupid name. He's even more annoying than you.'

'Thank you, I'm going to take that as a compliment.'

'You shouldn't. It wasn't one.'

'Anyway – have a look at him over there by the gazebo.'

We both looked over to where Pushatron 2000

was picking up litter. (Who does that at lunchtime, I mean really?) He had a black bin bag and was walking between groups of kids chatting and playing, collecting rubbish from the playground floor.

For once, Jess's expression changed from its usual frown of moody-slash-disgustedness to one of surprise. 'He's not pushing anyone!'

'Exactly, Jessticles, exactly. Let's go and find out why.'

I walked casually up to Pushatron. 'Hey, why are you on litter patrol?'

'Good afternoon, friend! I'm just doing my bit to keep our school in a tip-top state. A tidy school is a happy school!'

'Oh, defos. But wouldn't you rather be doing something else, though? Maybe … pushing someone?'

'Goodness, no. There's no need to push and shove, instead let's hug and share the love.'

He came at me and Jess with his arms wide open. Jess looked horrified and backed away, so I had to sacrifice myself and let him put his arms around me while I sort of patted his back. It was pretty awkward.

'Thanks for the hug, kid. It was extra-squeezy, just how I like them.'

'Anytime, friend!' And the kid formerly known as Pushatron 2000 went back to picking up empty crisp packets.

'Just one more thing … just to clarify: nobody made you spend your lunchtime picking up rubbish? You're doing it because you want to?'

'Oh yes, after all, a tidy school is…'

'A happy school, yeah, we got that,' Jess interrupted. Honestly, that girl is not good at pretending to be nice to people so that you can get what you want from them. Non-pushing Pushatron didn't seem to take offence though, he just stood there smiling and nodding. That is until Marek from Year 4, a.k.a. The Sniffler, ran past and a screwed-up tissue fell out of his pocket onto the floor. Newly named Hugatron 2000's face dropped into an expression of shock and devastation, like someone had just run over his puppy. The kid looked crushed. He stared at The Sniffler's back for a moment, in a world of his own, and then suddenly seemed to snap out of it.

'Excuse me, friend, I must get back to my duties,' he said and ran off.

'So that was super-weird,' I said to Jess as we watched him scurry after the snotty tissue, blowing gently across the playground.

'I think your stink is getting better – I couldn't smell anything, even when he was lying about picking up rubbish for fun.'

'My stink isn't getting better, Jess, my stink is as stinky as it has ever been. That's the weirdest part of all: he wasn't lying. Something has happened to that kid. Something has totally changed him.'

'Something or someone?'

'That's a very good question.'

7

I Am The King Of Stealth.
And Door Safety.

From then on we both watched the kids closely.
We watched them in class: always arriving precisely
two minutes early and laying out their books and
pencil cases on the table in the exact same way.
Sometimes we messed with them by 'accidentally'
bumping into their desks, making their books all
wonky. For a second, they would look panicked,
but then they'd put everything back where it was
and smile.

During PALS they all seemed to go into a trance. They sat neatly on the floor, eyes forward, gazing at the screen. Whatever happened around them, they didn't take their eyes off it. Sometimes people pass around notes during PALS, but if someone tried to pass anything to one of these kids, they were completely ignored. If anyone threw something at one of them, because they didn't pass on a note, the kid would just carry on sitting perfectly still. One time, Carrie-Anne Clarke got hit hard in the face with half a Jaffa cake, and she didn't even flinch. It was like she was hypnotised. And all the time they smiled. But their smiles were unnatural, like the way my mum smiles at Nanny Sparrow when she's telling Mum how to make a better Yorkshire pudding.

The time when it was hardest to watch them was at breaks. We'd see one or two on litter duty, but the rest of them seemed to disappear.

'They must be going somewhere,' Jess said. 'If we knew where, it might give us a clue about what's happening to them.'

'I'll find out where. I just need some night-vision goggles small enough to conceal in my hat, an infra-red camera, caretaker's overalls...'

'Or we could just follow one of them,' said Jess.

I looked at her. 'I'd better be the one to do that.'

'Why you?'

'Because I have years of stealth training under my belt.'

'Really? Where did you do that?' Jess raised an eyebrow.

'At the Awesome Agent Alex Academy. Or as I like to call it: Aaaaaaa.'

'I'm guessing this organisation is based at some top-secret location. Or, as I like to call it, your house.'

'Maybe. Maybe not. You'll never know because you're not stealthy enough to get in,' I said. 'Your dumb boots are the enemy of stealth.'

'They might be the enemy of stealth but they're best friends with kicking-annoying-people-in-the-shins.'

'Quiet, Jessticles, I'm running through my list of potential targets… I'm pretty sure Carrie-Anne Clarke in my class is one of them; she's always been a suck-up, but lately she's taken it to another level. And she doesn't believe in *Frozen* anymore. I'll see where she goes at afternoon break and meet you at the rendezvous point at fourteen-hundred hours.'

'Why are you speaking in that weird voice?'

'It's my secret-agent voice, obvs.' Honestly, Jess was so clueless sometimes.

'Right. And the rendezvous point is?'

'The Throne of Whispers in the Isolation Zone,' I said.

'See you at the Friendship Bench at two, then, Double-O-Dufus.'

I was super-excited about my first proper stealth mission. I wouldn't get to use my power, but I could test out some of my other spying skills.

At the end of class, Carrie-Anne packed her things away, stood up without scraping her chair across the floor like the rest of us do, and tucked the chair under the table. She wasn't taking much notice of what was going on around her, but this was supposed to be a stealth mission, and I wasn't going to let her take that away from me.

I followed her down the corridor, being sure to maintain a safe distance between us. (Twenty metres according to the AAAA handbook. Yes, there's a handbook.) I tiptoed past the library, where the floor is squeaky (a good agent knows his terrain) and stopped to take a reccy before I reached the IT hub.

I peeped around the corner just in time to see her turning right towards the art cupboard, so then I had to run to catch up, which wasn't my stealthiest moment. She started to turn her head, so I had to duck into a classroom, where Mrs Cobb and Mrs Halloway from the school office were eating Hobnobs.

'Sorry, I thought this was the boys' toilets!' I said as I hurried out again, leaving them with a bit of a stink.

Keeping Carrie-Anne in sight, I stayed close to the wall as I slunk, like a panther, down the corridor which led all the way to the far end of the school. To the PALS suite. The PALS suite is a new part of the school that literally popped up over the summer holidays. It was all shiny and colourful and kind of stood out from the rest of the school. It had a classroom, a couple of smaller rooms for quiet reflection, Smilie's office and the main PALS room. The best thing about it was the giant aquarium in the big room, full of tropical fish and coral.

Carrie-Anne opened the door and went inside, followed by maybe fifteen other kids. They were from different classes and year groups but they all walked with straight backs, chins up and eyes ahead. There were no hands in pockets or untucked shirts; no flashes of colour under trouser legs from forbidden non-grey socks. None of the girls had bows in their hair.

I hesitated at the double doors. This was Miss Smilie's domain. I wanted to see what the kids were doing in there but Smilie was super-strict. Come on, Agent Alex, I thought, you'll never get into S.H.I.E.L.D. if you're frightened of opening a door. I reached for the handle, just as the door opened from the inside.

'Alex Sparrow,' Miss Smilie smiled at me, 'to what do we owe this visit? Have you come to join us?'

Don't panic. Think fast. 'As much as I'd love to, Miss, I was actually just testing these doors.'

'Testing the doors?'

'Yes. I'm very concerned about health and safety, you see, and I'd heard reports that these new doors had loose handles that are likely to fall off and cause an accident.' I yanked on the handle and tried to wiggle it a bit to prove my point, hoping I'd somehow acquired a bit of super-strength along with my farting ear. It didn't budge.

'I haven't heard anything about faulty door handles, though if health and safety is a priority of yours, perhaps you could do some research on the causes of unpleasant odours. I've noticed a bad smell around the school.'

She looked at me, her eyes cold, and I had to resist the urge to shudder. She couldn't know about me, could she? It was impossible.

'Are you sure you wouldn't like to come in?' she said. 'The PALS suite is the perfect place for a boy like you. Once you've tried it you'll be coming here every day, I guarantee it.' It seemed a weird thing to say, because clearly there were a million things I'd rather do than go to the PALS suite every day, but she wasn't lying.

I heard a loud nose-blow behind me and Miss Smilie's smile stretched wider than before. She was wearing red lipstick and for a moment I thought it looked like blood smeared over her lips. Ridic, obviously. It was just lipstick.

'Ah, Marek, you're two minutes late.'

'Sorry, Miss Smilie.' It was The Sniffler, looking even paler than he usually did.

'I have plans for you – some quiet reflection on the evils of dropping litter.'

'Yes, Miss Smilie.'

I felt sorry for The Sniffler but not enough to hang around the PALS suite any longer. Besides, quiet reflection was boring as daytime TV, but it wouldn't kill him.

'I'd best be off, Miss, so I can investigate this terrible smell. First stop: the staffroom.'

I turned away.

'Hold on, please, Alex.'

Bums. I turned back, half expecting Miss Smilie to have grown tentacles so she could wrap them around me and pull me in.

'Yes, Miss?'

'Hats off in the school building.'

I was so relieved not to be dragged into the PALS suite, that I didn't argue, just pulled my hat off, stuffed it in my pocket and walked away as quickly as I could without running. I didn't look back.

8

I (Reluctantly) Become
The Apprentice

'It's quite hard at first, but once you've got it and have practised a bit, you'll start doing it automatically.'

I'd filled Jess in on what happened at the PALS suite and, while we tried to decide what to do next, we had other work to keep us busy. Apparently while I hadn't managed to get any control over my power, Jess had. So annoying.

'Look, no offence, Jess, but if you managed it, I'm sure I can.'

'Let's not forget that I'm the one who worked out how to do it, while you ran around stinking up the place,' said Jess, screwing up her nose.

'Well, excuse me for using my power for something actually fun.' I rolled my eyes.

'Yeah, that part where you humiliated yourself in front of your whole class sounded like a LOT of fun.'

'Low blow, Jess. You should be glad – if my friends didn't temporarily hate me, you wouldn't get to hang out with me.'

'Because I've got nothing better to do…'

'Exactly, you'd probably just be drawing skull tattoos on your arms.'

'Better that than spending time with a bunch of kids who only like you if you agree with everything they say.'

'There's nothing wrong with joining in, it's what normal people do.'

'Who wants to be normal?'

'It's better than being laughed at. Why would you want people to call you a freak?'

Jess glared at me. For a moment I thought she was going to punch me, but she just sighed and said, in her most bossy voice, 'Shall we get started?'

'Yeah, alright. Chill out, Jessticles.'

'All you have to do is concentrate. You need to block out the sounds around you so that your ears focus on just the person you're choosing to listen to.'

'Like a filter?'

'Yeah, exactly. Why are you laughing?'

'Just picturing you spasming out in the middle of PALS in front of the whole school.'

'How would it happen in PALS, you idiot? See many cows wandering around in the school hall do you? Monkeys swinging from the beams in the gym?' Jess glared at me.

'Can my filter be a Jess filter?'

'Do you want my help or not?'

'Yes. Sorry. Carry on.'

'So what you have to do is imagine your ears being blocked and only allowing certain things through. It helped me to actually visualise a little wall inside my ear.'

'What is your wall made of? Bricks?'

'No. Cloud.'

'You have a wall in your ear made of cloud?'

'Yes, and when I want to let a voice in, the cloud forms a little hole for the sound to squeeze through.'

'Right, got you. But I don't think I can have a cloud – it isn't very manly.'

'And you are, without doubt, the manliest boy I've ever come across.'

'I know, right? Can my wall be made of something a bit more superheroey, like iron or kryptonite?'

'Whatever works for you.'

'Ok, I'm going with adamantium.'

'Because you're just like Wolverine.'

'Yes. Yes, I am.'

'OK, so when there are voices around you, imagine the ones you don't want to hear bouncing off the adamantian wall in your ear.'

'God, Jess, it's adamantiUM, not adamantiAN. Fancy getting something so important wrong. Next you'll be calling me Alan and that is clearly not the name of a super spy.'

'It would be perfect for you, then.'

'Ooh, you are extra ragey today! What's the matter? Did Big Darth D ditch you for a girl who doesn't just talk about orphans and despair?'

'Can we just get on with this?'

'Fine, keep your wig on. What do I do with the voices I want to let through?'

'You could imagine the adamantium melting to make a gap.'

'Unlikely. Adamantium's molecular structure is so stable that it can't be moulded, even if the temperature is high enough to keep it liquified. Your Marvel knowledge is appalling, Jessticles.'

'So how will you let the voices through, geek-boy?'

'My wall will retract.'

'Wolverine'd better watch out – he's got some serious competition now. Alan and his retractable adamantian ear-wall.'

'Shut up.'

'So now you know how it's done, you can start practising.'

We wandered around the playground, passing groups of kids having the usual conversations, which I knew by now were made up of a lot of fibs. Kids' lies usually fell into one of two categories. The first was denial: 'I definitely do not want Nadine Skelton to be my girlfriend. She's so annoying!' or 'I never kicked your football over the fence, but I saw Khalil running off – it was probably him.' The second type was the showing-off lie: 'I completed the new Lego game in one day.' You get the idea. There were some kids who seemed to lie all the time, which I would have expected. What surprised me was that pretty much everybody lied sometimes, even if it was not very often. So the playground was a minefield for me – ear-fart bombs exploding at every turn, especially without my hat on. It was a good place to practise.

'I guess Rhys from 6P really does want Nadine Skelton to be his girlfriend, then,' Jess said, after my ear popped one out for the millionth time. It was so frustrating.

'You mean The Golden Rhys? Yeah, he does, the nutter. She's so bossy – she'll have him finger-knitting and making jewellery out of old sweet wrappers before he realises what's happening.'

Usually at break we went to the quiet parts of the playground, away from anything that would activate our powers. Having my ear buzzing away constantly was giving me a headache. I suddenly felt tired and sad.

'I'm really not getting the hang of this filtering thing, am I? I totally reek. Sorry.' I wouldn't blame Jess if she ditched me.

She stopped walking. 'Alex, you have nothing to

apologise for. This situation is new and difficult and not your fault. Some people would moan and give up, but you're trying hard to make the best of it. The smell isn't even that bad now that I'm used to it.'

Blimey! What happened to the real Jess? I was going to thank her, but I was distracted by the sight of a familiar person heading our way.

'Oh, man. It's Jason.'

'Your former best mate? Great.'

'We're going to walk right past each other. I'll have to say hi. Don't do or say anything embarrassing.'

And there he was, giving a finger swear to a Reception kid who accidentally bumped him with his violin case.

'Hi, Jason.'

I thought he might just ignore me, but he actually looked happy to see me. Maybe he was going to ask me over for pancakes and PS4. Maybe he had really missed me and wanted to be my best mate again.

'Scuzzo! I was just going to check the bottom of my shoe, thinking I'd stepped in something. Should have known it was you. You smell worse than dog's turds.'

OK, maybe not.

'How's things? Are you going to see the new X-Men movie?'

'I saw that movie ages ago, loser. Nice girlfriend, by the way, she looks like a total freak.'

'Jess is *so* not my girlfriend.'

'Yeah, she is. Scuzzo's got a freakish ugly girlfriend!' (He said that bit in an annoying 'na na na-na na' voice.) 'Best you could do I guess, seeing as you're a stinking loser.'

Insulting me was one thing, but saying that stuff about Jess was really making me mad. Jess was precisely the only person at school who was being a friend to me. Well, her and Darth Daver. Jason could be such a massive jerk.

'Shut up, Jason. She's not ugly and she's not a freak!'

'Really? What the hell is she doing then?'

Jess was in the middle of a full-on, hardcore twitch. I'd seen it a few times now, but it was still entertaining and there was always the hope that she might take it to the next level. I had my fingers crossed for her to mutate into She-Hulk and throw Jason over the fence.

I soon spotted the cause of her outburst: Dexter

the pigeon was on the ground beside us, strutting about like a boss. I was a bit annoyed by the timing. I didn't need to give Jason any more reasons to disown me. But then Dexter hated me because I mocked his disability, so he probably did it on purpose.

Jason looked horrified. 'You dropped your tramp hat,' he said, throwing it at me and walking away. He clearly didn't want to be seen with us. 'Don't ever come near me again, Scuzzo,' Jason shouted. 'Stupid, stinking freaks!'

Jess stopped twitching as Dexter flew away, making sure to land a sloppy poo on my head as he left. I was wearing my hat, though, so it didn't get in my hair. Joke's on him.

'So?' I said.

'He said The Professor wants an update on what we've found out so far. Apparently we're supposed to write it down on a little piece of paper, roll it up and tie it to Dexter's leg so he can deliver it by the end of lunch.'

'The Professor really needs to get an email address. I didn't hear you agreeing to anything.'

'That's because I didn't. I'm not taking orders from someone who doesn't have the balls to give them himself.'

I gasped. 'You said balls!'

Jess rolled her eyes.

'So we're going rogue! Awesome!' There's nothing cooler than a rogue agent. 'Agent Alex and his trusty sidekick, The Living Zombie, throw off the chains of authority and take matters into their own hands.'

'You're doing another absurd voice. Are you *narrating* our situation?'

'The Living Zombie hides her respect for Agent Alex under a veil of contempt.'

'Stop referring to me as The Living Zombie.'

'Why? You need a sidekick name and it makes you sound like a bad-A.'

'Think of something else.'

'Aha! So you *want* a sidekick name!'

'I didn't say that.'

'You didn't have to, I think we understand each other,' I said.

Jess looked as though she wanted to slap me, so it was the perfect time for a subject change. 'What else did Dexter say? You were twitching for ages.'

'Something about watching out for dodgy geezers who are giving it the large, and not messing with the boss.'

'Ooh, do you think there's a band of highly trained gangland criminals on our tails?'

'Because Cherry Tree Lane is full of gangland criminals.' Jess rolled her eyes.

'The trouble with you, Jessticles, is that you have no imagination.'

'The trouble with you, Agent Alex, is that you have too much.'

We walked in silence for a few minutes to give my ear a break.

'Oh, I just got it,' Jess said. 'The Golden Rhys – like the Golden Fleece because of his hair. That's actually not bad.'

'Duh!'

9

Banished

After a quick visit to the boys' toilets to wash the poo off my hat, I was almost glad to go back to class after lunch. My head was ringing from all the lie-detecting, and from concentrating so hard on making my adamantium filter work. I always knew that being a spy involved a lot of risks, but I thought the pain would come from being thrown into a pool of mutated giant squid, not from having a farting ear.

'Alex Sparrow, will you please pay attention. Or

perhaps you think you can just ignore everything I say?'

Miss Fortress was standing over me, looking even more flustered than usual. I was not in the mood for a fight.

'No, Miss Fortress, sorry. I'm listening.'

'Really? Because it seems to me that you think you can make up your own rules.'

'I don't think that. I really don't. It's just...'

'It's just insolent and ungrateful and I don't know why I bother trying to help you children, when you have no appreciation of all the brilliant work I do.'

She was getting red in the face and her hair, which had been piled up on top of her head, was falling down and flapping about like a deranged lion's mane. She was totally freaking out. What the heck had I done to annoy her so much? Miss Smilie already had it in for me, and now Miss Fortress was at it. Come to think of it, Fortress had started teaching at the school at around the same time Smilie did. Perhaps they were working together. Perhaps they were the ones changing the kids. Time to get some answers.

'What makes you say that, Miss Fortress?'

She seemed a bit taken aback by my question. The whole class went silent and looked at her, waiting to see how she'd react.

'You were daydreaming and not participating in my lesson.'

'But you seem *extremely* annoyed with me. Is that the only reason?'

'Yes, of course.' She snapped back at me.

Big. Fat. Liar.

'So I've not done anything else wrong, other than having a very small and insignificant moment of not paying full attention in class?'

'No.' Another lie.

'So don't you think you're overreacting a bit then?'

I knew I was playing a dangerous game, but the more I pushed her, the more mad she got; and the more mad she got, the more she gave away. Just as I thought she was about to explode, she suddenly stopped and took a deep breath. She walked over to the windows and started opening them, one by one, muttering about a bad smell. The anticipation was awful. The other kids were watching her, open-mouthed, probably calculating in their heads how many weeks of golden time –

a.k.a. the only time at school when you can do what you want and is actually fun – I was going to lose.

But she didn't take away my golden time. She tried to take away something much more important.

'Alex Sparrow, you will do as you are told in my classroom. Get back to work, and take that ghastly hat off.'

Not my hat. Please, not my hat. It was sad and desperate but after a lunchtime of constant ear-farting, my head was pounding, and I honestly believed my hat was the only thing keeping the stink from being completely out of control and my life from being over.

'But why, Miss?'

'Because you shouldn't be wearing a hat in the classroom. Perhaps your concentration will improve if you increase the amount of oxygen getting to your brain.'

Everyone laughed.

'I'm sorry, Miss Fortress. I'll pay attention…'

I was feeling picked on, and keeping my hat on had become a matter of pride.

From the other side of the room, Jason

shouted, 'Your hat looks like it came out of a bin, Scuzzo!'

More laughter.

'No hats in my classroom. Take it off now.'

Miss Fortress walked over to my desk. For one awful moment, I thought she was going to confiscate my hat. I felt totally outraged and also, though it sounds utterly pathetic, like I was going to cry.

'Don't get too close, Miss, you might catch his stink!'

'Be quiet, Jason. I'm sick of hearing your irritating voice.'

But the damage was done. The whole class was laughing at me. I hated Miss Fortress, really hated her.

'I'm not taking it off.'

'Then I don't want you in my classroom. Take your textbook and do some silent reading in the library.'

I picked up my stuff and walked out, to the sound of more abuse and name-calling and Miss Fortress trying to get the class back under control. I was so angry, at Smilie and Fortress, at Jason and Dexter, and at The Professor. The stupid lie detector was ruining my life.

The library was surprisingly busy. I didn't feel like reading about three-dimensional shapes, so I thought I'd have a little wander.

I sidled over to a table full of kids reading quietly. FYI, sidling is the way you walk when you're about to do something you shouldn't be doing and you don't want to draw attention to yourself. The kids were all smiling, so I figured they must be reading really good books.

'What you reading?' I asked a girl who was beaming at her book. She had a thin face with a long nose and dark hair tied back in a neat bun (before you think anything bad about me, I only know what buns are because of my sister and her ballet classes). She looked kind of familiar but I couldn't quite place her.

'Hello, friend! You know we shouldn't be talking in the library: peace and quiet are always best when there are words of wisdom to digest!'

She was talking like Pushatron. I instantly went into agent mode.

'Oh yes, I was just saying that earlier. In a minute I'm going to be totes quiet so I can digest some wisdom. Maybe I could read what you're reading – it looks like you're enjoying it.'

'I am, and I know you would too. It's the PALS handbook – you can get a copy from the shelf over there. It has a hundred new affirmations to learn!'

'Sounds awesome.'

'It's PALStastic! And I have golden time now, so I get to read it for a whole hour.'

Wait … what?! 'Let me get this straight: you're using your golden time to read a PALS handbook?'

'Yes, friend! If you don't mind, I must get back to my reading.'

Just like with Pushie, she wasn't lying. She really was using her golden time to read a boring PALS book in the library. Who the heck was this girl? It was only then that I recognised her: it was Saira from 3M. We called her The Whip because she wore her hair in a massive plait down her back and used it to slap boys who annoyed her. Well, she wasn't The Whip anymore. There was no way she could attack anyone with her bun.

I looked down the table and saw that all the kids were reading PALS books. I moved on to the next table and they were doing the same. I was about to sidle away before someone tried to make me read the PALS handbook when I spotted The Sniffler.

'Hey, Marek, how was your detention with Smilie?'

'Hello, friend! It was wonderful – it left me with a smile on my face and a song in my heart.'

Oh no. Poor Sniffler was one of them. It had only just happened though. Maybe I could snap him out of it.

'I see you're reading the PALS handbook there, Marek. It's an excellent book, but can I recommend something else? We could read it together.'

I grabbed one of my favourite books from a nearby shelf. 'This book is epic. It has a fight between a yeti and a vampire.'

Sniffler looked alarmed. 'No thank you, friend.'

'OK, OK … well can I interest you in pirates? Everyone loves a pirate: all that plundering and sword fighting.'

Sniffler rubbed his face with his hands. 'I must get back to my handbook.'

'Got it! You want something with evil robots…'

Sniffler was leaving finger marks on his cheeks where he was rubbing them so hard. He was starting to shake.

'Magic trees? Swamp monsters? Zombie cowboys?'

Sniffler covered his ears and screamed, 'Stop it! Stop it! Stop it!'

The other PALS kids gathered round him. 'When you're feeling sad and glum,' The Whip said, 'it's always great to hug a chum.' She put her arms around him.

I started backing away, just as Jess walked in with a book in her hand.

'Why is that kid freaking out?' she whispered.

'Well…'

'You did something to him, didn't you?' She looked at me and huffed.

I pulled her over to an empty corner of the library. 'Do you see what all those kids are reading?'

Jess peered around the bookshelf and raised an eyebrow. 'Are they PALS handbooks?'

'Yes. And get this: all those kids are on golden time.'

Jess's mouth dropped open to form a perfect little 'o'.

'My thoughts exactly, Jessticles,' I said.

'So what's with the boy's meltdown? Did he just realise he's turned into a total lamo?'

'I tried to get him to look at some other books.'

'Something weird or controversial? I didn't think they kept that type of stuff in here.' Jess looked round at the library with what I'm pretty sure was a look of surprised delight.

'Of course not. Just stories. Stuff about monsters and magic.'

'And he freaked out?'

We both looked over at Sniffler who was trying to curl up in a ball under the table.

'Pretty much.'

'So maybe the PALS can't handle the thought of reading something that isn't PALS approved,' Jess said.

'Maybe. There's definitely a clue here, we just need to work out exactly what it is.'

Jess nodded. I love it when she agrees with me. Obviously I am always right, but usually she's too angry-slash-annoying to realise.

'What are you doing in here anyway?' I asked her.

'Just returning this.' She held up a book called *The Human Brain*.

'You're so weird.'

'I got it for research, dummy. I thought it might

help us to work out what's happening to the PALS kids, and maybe what happened to us, too.'

'You're such a swot. You could have investigated in a much more exciting way, like by breaking into a brain-research facility, but instead you did a Hermione. If anyone can make secret-agenting seem dull, it's you, Jess.'

'At least I'm doing something useful and not moping around the library in a bad mood.'

'So I suppose you've solved the case then: you and your library book of wonder.'

'I found out a lot about brain experimentation.'

That sounded quite evil and exciting. 'What sort of experimentation?'

'Lobotomies, for example.'

'What's a robotomy? Is that the thing where robots take over the world and make humans their slaves? Do you think Miss Smilie is the head robot? That would explain a lot.'

'Not robotomy, lobotomy. It's a surgical procedure they used to do in the old days where they cut out bits of people's brains to try to change their personalities.'

What?! Doctors cut out bits of people's brains? That's horrific!

'Oh, yeah, lobotomy. Totally knew that.'

'Course you did.' Jess did a small but deliberate sniff. 'Mmmm, eggy.'

'What else?'

'Well, there's also this electric shock therapy thing…'

'We got shocked by The Professor!'

'We did. The electric shock in the ear is obviously what gave us our powers.'

'So we're a couple of bad-As, like Electro,' I said.

'Except we don't have blue skin and we haven't rampaged through New York.'

'Exactly, Jessticles.' A sudden, exciting thought hit me. 'If an electric shock gave us our powers, I wonder if it could take them away too?'

'I guess it's possible, but we'd need to find out from someone who knows a lot more about it.' She looked me hard in the eyes. 'It is definitely not something that you or I should try to do on our own.'

Well, that's what she said, but what I heard was 'It is definitely ~~not~~ something that you ~~or I~~ should do ~~on our own~~.'

'I have to get back to class,' she said, 'I'll see you at break.'

'Yeah, cool, cool. See you at break.'

She frowned at me and left. Life had got so complicated since I bought the lie detector. All my friends hated me, Miss Fortress was giving me a hard time, and Miss Smilie probably wanted to PALSify me. I wished I could go back to how things were before.

I checked that the coast was clear and then started sliding across the floor between the bookshelves. It was kind of like ice-skating, but on beige carpet and in my school shoes, which were perfect because they had slippy soles. I slid and slid and slid some more, being careful not to fall because the library carpet had 'friction burns' written all over it. I HATE friction burns, especially when they go gooey and Mum puts cream on them. There is no greater pain. So, anyway, I skidded around and after about ten minutes I decided to take the plunge. Still sliding, I approached one of those stands that holds leaflets – you know, stuff about not talking to strangers on the internet, not playing on train tracks, not riding your bike without a helmet. I couldn't see a leaflet about 'not giving yourself an electric shock on a leaflet stand in order to get rid of a lie detector you were tricked into buying', so I bent down and put my ear to the metal. I felt a sharp shock as my ear made contact. I let out a little yelp and jumped back, right into Miss Kaur, the librarian and Miss Fortress. Damn.

'I'll leave you to deal with this, Hope,' Miss Kaur said, walking over to Marek's table. (Hope was Miss Fortress's human name.)

'What exactly are you doing, Alex?' Miss Fortress said, looking at my ear, which was feeling quite sore.

'I was just, um, practising my moves.' My little fib made my ear poot: the static shock hadn't worked.

'I was hoping you'd use your time in the library for something more productive,' she said. 'If you've quite finished, you'd better get back to class. Miss Kaur doesn't want you in here causing any more disruption.'

I walked behind her back to the classroom, wondering how I'd managed to get myself in so much trouble. Things had got super-tense, and I was going to have to be more careful now that I had both Smilie and Fortress breathing down my neck.

10

Introducing Agent Bob

'One of us is going to have to go undercover.'

Jess and I were trying to think of a way to get into the PALS suite so we could find out what was happening in there to make the kids so mental.

'Don't look at me,' Jess said, 'I'd rather rub peri-peri in my eyes than pretend to be a PALS pal.'

'Actually, you're right. I can't think of a single person who would do a worse job. You'd have to lie. You'd have to speak politely to people you despise, and you'd have to smile.'

'I can smile!'

'Come on, Jess, we both know you only smile when you're with DD or when you're starting a petition about something.'

'Well, thanks to you running around peeing off half the kids in PALS, you'll never get in with them. Miss Smilie and Miss Fortress are suspicious of you already.'

'What we need is a grappling hook, a can of hairspray and a digital recording device.'

'What we need is someone small and quiet who can hide easily and who we can trust not to sell us out to anyone,' said Jess.

'I know we can trust Darth Daver, but he's as tall as a giraffe!'

'I didn't mean Dave, dufus – I know the perfect person.'

Jess leant on my breakfast bar so that she was nose to nose with Bob. 'Please, Bob. We'll make it worth your while.'

We'd been working on Bob for the best part of an hour. We figured that if we could put him in a little jar of water and plant it somewhere in the PALS room, he'd be able to watch and report back to us. He was worried about getting caught. And, more importantly, he was worried about the disruption to his routine. We'd tried flattering him. We'd tried begging him. The only thing left was bribery.

I stood a bit further back, wondering if there was any way a goldfish could leap out of the water and projectile poo on me.

'Tell him he can have anything he wants.'

'He says he doesn't want anything.'

'A bigger tank – tell him he can have a bigger tank.'

'I don't need to tell him, Alex, he can hear you. And he wants the tank he has now. He's got it just the way he likes it.'

I really couldn't get my head round the animals-understanding-me thing. But more importantly, how the heck had he got his tank the way he liked it? Did he stay up after everyone went to bed rearranging the gravel at the bottom?

'What about a little statue of a mermaid or one of those cool castle things?'

'He says they'll ruin the feng shui.'

'More food, what about more food?'

'He says, "Are you mocking me?"'

'What? No! Why would I be mocking him?'

'He thinks we think he's fat.'

'Oh my God. That's all we need – a paranoid goldfish.'

'He said he isn't paranoid. He distinctly heard you discussing it with your family a few weeks ago.'

'What? He's crazy!'

'He said it occurred on a Saturday morning at 9:16. You entered the room first, followed by the small girl who always presses her face on his walls and leaves nasty smears. He remembers it precisely because it was the morning that you first started acting in a bizarre manner.'

'Oh – *that* morning.'

'Did you call him fat?'

'No. Not exactly. I called him "fatter" than the old goldfish.'

'Nice one Double-O-Dufus.'

'Well, how was I supposed to know that one day I'd be asking him to spy on a psychopath and her freaky minions in the PALS suite for me?'

'Hold on, he has another question… He wants to know what happened to the previous occupant of his tank?'

'Oh, er, that's a bit of a long story.'

'He says he has time.'

'The old Miley had a little accident involving some Red Bull.'

Jess looked at me, eyes wide. 'What kind of accident?'

'Well, she was a very different kind of person, I mean fish. She was always leaping about all over the place, throwing herself around willy-nilly. And one day I left some Red Bull next to her tank. The nutter jumped out of the water and dived right in! I tried to save her, gave her the kiss of life and everything, but it was no use.'

Jess sniffed the air and raised an eyebrow. I couldn't tell Bob the truth though, could I? Seriously, what would you do in that situation?

'He said she sounds like a lunatic.'

'Oh, yes, she was.'

'But that doesn't change the fact that you called him fat.'

'I'm sorry. What can I do?'

'He's thought of something we can do in exchange for him providing the services we've discussed.'

'Brilliant. What is it?'

Jess twitched away for a bit and then looked at me, completely deadpan and said, 'He wants to go on a special diet he's heard about. It requires that he only eats one colour of food at a time. A different colour each day. He wants us to separate his food into different colours and make sure he only gets one colour of flake per day. Starting with green, then orange, yellow, blue, brown, back to green and so on.'

'Are you serious?'

'He's always serious.'

'Have you seen his food?'

'No, why?'

'It's a pot of millions of tiny paper-thin flakes in lots of colours, all mixed up together. It will take hours to separate them. Hours!'

Jess sighed. 'You get the food and I'll get some tweezers.'

Our first job was to transfer Bob into a washed-out coffee jar with holes in the lid that we'd prepared the night before. When I say prepared, I mean we spent about an hour following his endless instructions: 'Make sure you scrub it at least three times with a mild detergent, if there's any coffee residue in there, it could bring on a migraine. Rinse it out properly, at least five times, any detergent residue could result in a severe allergic reaction. Make sure the air holes are large and evenly spaced, if they are too small, or not lined up symmetrically, it could cause a sudden painful death…' You get the picture.

To be fair, it must have been quite scary for him, leaving his comfortable tank and being sent on a dangerous mission.

'Ah, bless him, poor little chap. Do you think he knows what he's getting himself into? Those crazy PALS could be capable of anything.'

'For God's sake, Alex.'

'What?'

'I can't even bring myself to say it again.'

'What?'

She looked down at Bob in his Nescafé jar and then she looked at me, *both* eyebrows raised.

'Oh, bums! Sorry, Bob, I forgot you could hear… I mean, I was only joking about the crazy PALS kids – there's no way they'd do anything to hurt you.'

There was an awkward silence while Bob stared at me.

'Will he still help us?'

'He's weighed up his options and thinks it's worth the risk. Statistics prove that there are more obesity-related deaths than cult-related deaths. The odds are in his favour.'

'Fair play, Bob. You strange, strange little fish.'

The best time to get Bob into position was at the very beginning of the lunch hour, while Smilie and the PALS were eating in the canteen. We were lucky, the PALS suite was open and the coast was clear. I found a great hiding place for Bob, up on a high shelf in the main room, behind a load of musical instruments. We made sure he was comfortable and had a good view of the room and quietly left.

Jess looked worried. 'Do you think he'll be OK?'

'Yeah, I'm sure he will. He was quite happy in his jar and he was well hidden. They won't find him.'

'I feel bad. Like we've exploited him or something. Maybe we should hand ourselves in to the RSPCA.'

'Bob knew the risks. He's a soldier. He'll be fine.'

I tried to reassure Jess, but I felt pretty worried

myself. Lunch dragged by, until finally it was time to go and pick him up.

Collecting Bob was more risky. The PALS left the suite four minutes before afternoon registration, which left only a window of three minutes to get Bob and return to our classrooms. We watched them file out and then made our move.

The PALS room was exactly as we'd left it. I was almost disappointed.

'It doesn't look like anything weird has been going on in here,' I said.

'What were you expecting to find? Ropes and gags? Some blood spatters on the floor? Maybe some booklets called *How to Survive a Lobotomy*?'

Yes. 'No, of course not.'

'We'd better get out of here before your stink gives us away.'

I climbed up to the shelf and was happy to see Bob swimming very small circuits around his jar. I passed him down to Jess and she hid him in her bag. Just in time.

'Alex Sparrow and Jessica Lawler. Why aren't I surprised to see you again?'

We both turned to see Miss Smilie standing by

the door. Perfect. How did she always know where I was? We needed to get away – when people got stuck in the PALS suite with Smilie, they came out different. I had to get us out of this. I might have a defective ear and an odour issue, but I was still Agent Alex. I had skills and tactics. I had street smarts. And above all else I was an expert in winding people up.

'It *is* a bit odd that we keep bumping into each other,' I said. 'To be honest, it's getting awkward. I have to ask: are you following me?'

'That is beyond ridiculous – why would I be following you?'

She'd avoided answering the question. 'We could call it "keeping an eye on me" if you're more comfortable with that?'

'I am not keeping an eye on you.'

'Something tells me you are.'

'I have no interest in impudent boys with smart mouths.'

'It's OK, Miss, I get it: I'm a very charismatic person. Most people want to be close to me. Jess was the same; that's how we became friends, isn't it, Jess?'

Jess just stared at me and did a tiny shake of the head. She was seriously no help in these situations.

'You're not supposed to be in here. What are you doing?' Smilie was still smiling but I could tell she was annoyed.

'Well, first we came to make sure your door handles hadn't dropped off,' I said, looking around and trying to think up a convincing excuse. The shelf of musical instruments caught my eye. 'And then we came into the PALS room, because we're, erm, starting a band.'

'Well, that's wonderful news! And what instruments do you play?'

'Jess plays the recorder and I'm the singer.'

'As fabulous as that sounds, it still doesn't explain why you are here and why you are climbing up to that top shelf.'

'Yes, but I can explain that. We needed some stuff for our band.' I grabbed the two closest things from the shelf. 'One of these tambourines and some, erm, music, the music, on this paper, for a song we want to do.'

'He means the sheet music for a song we're covering.'

Thanks for your help, Jess. Could have done with some input a little bit earlier.

Miss Smilie put her hands on her hips and

smiled again. All teeth and lipstick. She looked like something out of *Doctor Who* that was about to swallow us whole.

'And what song are you going to be covering?'

I looked down at the sheet music and tried to act casual. It wouldn't have been my first choice but at least it worked with the tambourine.

'"If You're Happy And You Know It": the PALS remix.'

'I wouldn't have thought that would be quite your style, Jessica?'

Jess rolled her eyes and said, again in her most scathing, sarcastic tone, 'It's my favourite.'

Smilie's gaze fixed on Jess. I swear she was going to open her mouth at any second and gobble her up. So I tried to divert her attention.

'Come on, Miss, join in:

'If you're happy and you know it, hug a PAL; if you're happy and you know it, hug a PAL...' I sang as enthusiastically as I could, and rattled the tambourine. I was hoping Jess would join in but she just stood there looking appalled. She was a flipping useless sidekick.

Miss Smilie took a step towards us. 'You know, we have a musical group in PALS and we are *always* looking for new members. You two should join. We're all pals in PALS.'

We were doomed.

The bell rang for afternoon registration. Smilie's face went back to normal.

'You two had better go to your classrooms. And next time you want to borrow school equipment, ask permission.'

'Yes, Miss.'

We half ran out of the music block. When I turned to look behind, Smilie was still watching us.

11

She Wants To Eat Your Brain

We had to wait until after school to talk to Bob and find out what had happened in the PALS suite. When we got to my house, Jess tipped Bob back into his tank and I sprinkled his food (green flakes only) into the water. We waited until he'd finished his dinner and gone back to swimming his circuits and then we asked him what he'd seen.

'What happened in there, Bob?'

'He said there was nothing out of the ordinary.'

'How can that be?'

'I don't know, I'm just telling you what he said.'

'But that can't be right, it *can't* be. Ask him to run us through everything that went on.'

'OK… The kids went in, and then the lady with the bright red smile. The kids stood round the piano singing. They all smiled and gave themselves a clap when they finished each song.'

'Hang on, I'm still on bright red smile…'

'Are you writing this down?'

'Yes. In the mission log.'

'We have a mission log?'

'Of course we do. We don't want to forget anything, do we? And think how much the log will be worth to The Professor. I bet he'll take my power away in exchange for this little beauty.'

'Alex, that's a Cherry Tree Lane homework diary.'

'Exactly, it blends in, doesn't draw attention to itself. Also, I spent all of my pocket money on sausage rolls and the homework diary was free from the stationery cupboard in the school office. Please tell Bob to continue.'

'Twenty minutes in, the red smile lady said she had to collect a new member from the tasting room. She went to the end of the room; he couldn't see exactly where because his view was blocked. She came back a moment later with a boy.'

'Back-up a sec – what's the tasting room?'

'He doesn't know. But it must be close to the main room because she was only gone for a moment.'

'Bob, are you sure she said tasting room?'

'He said he couldn't hear very well so he had to lip-read. But he's ninety-nine per cent sure she said tasting room.'

'What happened next?'

'The other kids all smiled and cheered, but the new boy didn't smile back. He didn't say anything, just rubbed the side of his head.'

'That's weird. Then what?'

'They lined up and left in an orderly fashion.'

'So we have a boy coming out of a tasting room with a sore head? How is that nothing out of the ordinary, Bob?!'

'He said it was an hour of calm and structure, and seemed far more normal than the goings on in your house. The most alarming thing he saw was the giant aquarium. All those different fish sharing one tank doing whatever they liked and *living in the moment*. He says there didn't appear to be any kind of rota or timetable. He's quite upset about it.'

We were still leaning on the breakfast bar, watching Bob swimming round and round.

'Blimey.'

'I know I'm going to regret asking this,' Jess said, 'but what do you think was going on?'

'It's obvious – it can only be one thing. Smilie is an alien. She is eating the brains of the kids at school and replacing them with alien brains.'

'Oh yeah, obvious.'

'Do you have a better theory, Jessticles?'

'No, but brain-eating aliens isn't the first thing that comes to mind.'

'It's Smilie – she gives me the creeps.'

Jess stopped disagreeing with me for once. 'Smilie is creepy. No normal person smiles that much.'

'I don't even think it's proper smiling. She looks like a shark who's smelled blood.'

'So what do we do next? We need to find out where and what the tasting room is, but I think we ought to stay away from the PALS suite for a while. It's too dangerous.'

'Agreed. We can't go back there again. We'll have to find another way.'

12

Hacking the Mainframe

After Bob's successful mission, we were certain that Smilie was the big, bad baddie we were looking for. What we didn't know was why she was changing the kids, or how, or if anyone was helping her. We needed to find out more about her and Miss Fortress, who we suspected was her accomplice.

'If we could get a look at their files in the school records, that might tell us something.'

Even when Jess's ideas were good, they were

sensible and dull. It was lucky she had me to inject a bit of danger and excitement into them.

'We'll have to hack the mainframe.'

Jess sighed. 'And how are we going to do that?'

'All spies either have hacking abilities themselves, or a geeky associate who is an expert hacker. It's in all the books and all the movies.'

'I can't hack.'

'What do you mean, you can't hack? Now I'm going to have to stop calling you Web Master.'

'That won't be a problem.'

'Well, if you're going to be stubborn, we'll have to go old school. Agent Alex and his sidekick, Owlface, must risk their lives and their golden time, to break into a maximum security establishment…'

'First, you're narrating again. Second, Owlface? Really? And third, how are we going to break into the school office?'

'First, someone has to tell our story. Second, yes, because of your overly large eyes and spike nose, which is like a little beak. And third, I've had an idea but we'll need cunning disguises, preferably some prosthetics and a taser.'

'How about an idea we can use in the real world, rather than just in your head?'

'But it's do-able! We'll just have to find an expert make-up artist who is sympathetic to our cause, order a taser online…'

'And how much is a taser going to cost?'

'Well, I've seen one on American eBay for 400 dollars. That's only about £40.'

'Er, more like £250, idiot.'

'Really? Are you sure? Oh. Well I expect we can find a cheaper one.'

'No, Alex. No tasers. What a stupid plan.'

'Have a better one, do you?'

The following morning, the Life Coach was coming to school. It was basically a bunch of people who drove around in a special bus and put on plays about what to do if you're getting bullied, or why you shouldn't make prank 999 calls – stuff like that. They wore yellow baseball caps and thought they were totally down with the kids. The whole school had to watch the plays and go to workshops to discuss them. Usually it meant a morning without numeracy, which was pretty awesome, but this time it gave me and Jess the opportunity to carry out some serious recon.

Our plan was double pronged, so I decided to

call it 'Operation BOGOF'. While everyone in school was distracted, we were going to plant Bob in Miss Fortress's classroom so he could spy on her, while we broke into the head's office to get a look at the staff files. Putting Bob in place was easy once we'd convinced him to accept the mission. The school office was harder. There was just one person in our way – Mrs Cobb, the school secretary. She was a big lady. She was a mean lady. She really hated kids.

'Hello, Mrs Cobb. Lovely day.'

She didn't even answer me, just grunted and carried on with her typing.

'I wondered if I might speak to you for a moment about a little problem I've been having?'

'You need Mrs Halloway.' Mrs Halloway was the medical lady.

'Usually I would speak to Mrs Halloway, but I can't find her and this is urgent.'

'You'll have to wait for her. I'm not a first aider.'

'It really can't wait, you see, I've got bad diarrhoea.'

She looked up and I saw the glint of recognition in her eyes. She remembered my stink from the other day. She looked horrified.

'It started earlier this week and has been getting worse every day. My poo is really liquidy, like brown water and it burns as it comes out...'

She wheeled her chair a little further away from me.

'I must have spent half the morning sitting on the toilet. And every time the poo comes out, well, gushes out, it makes a lot of noise and the smell is disgusting...'

And of course, while I was telling such whopping lies, my ear was doing its job and creating a really bad smell.

'It's getting quite hard to stop it from, you know, coming out. I think I may have even stained my...'

Mrs Cobb jumped out of her chair and ran past me towards the door. 'I'll have to get Mrs Halloway.'

As soon as she was gone, Jess ran in.

'Good work, stinkboy.'

'We don't have much time. Where would the files be? Look in unlikely places and be ready to pick a lock.'

'How are we going to pick a lock?'

'With a hair-grip thingy. That's how everyone

does it on telly. Unless you have a sonic screwdriver, which I doubt.'

'I don't have a hair grip either, genius,' said Jess.

'Why not? You're a girl. Girls have hair grips.'

'Not all girls have hair grips to hand all of the time.'

'Call yourself a sidekick.' I stopped opening drawers and folded my arms in disgust.

'I have never called myself a sidekick.'

'I'm going to have to rethink your codename. You don't deserve to be called the Tiny Terror.'

'Shut up and keep looking,' said Jess, finding a moment to shoot me the side-eye of annoyance.

I went to the head's desk drawers, which were locked. 'I told you we'd need a hair grip.'

'We don't. I've found them. They were cunningly hidden in an unlocked drawer labelled "Staff Files".'

'Well done, Tiny Terror, I never would have thought of looking in such a boring hiding place.'

As I ran to the drawer, I swear I heard a scratching noise. My heart stopped.

'What's up?' Jess whispered.

'I heard something.'

'Like someone coming?'

'No. Something else.'

We both listened.

'I can't hear anything. You must have imagined it.'

'You can't hear it because it's stopped now. I'm not making it up – there was definitely something.'

'We'll have to worry about it later. Let's just copy the files we need and get out of here.'

We pulled out Fortress and Smilie's files, Jess photocopied the pages and I stuffed them in my pocket. I'm usually pretty chilled out, as you know, but for those few minutes in the office, even I started to panic. The photocopier was so slow and so noisy. And what we were doing was stuff you could get in proper trouble for. I was sure Mrs Cobb would come back and catch us, or that Smilie would suddenly appear. I had that horrible almost wetting yourself feeling, like when there's five minutes left at the end of a test and you're nowhere near finishing.

As soon as we were safely hidden in the girls' toilets, we pulled out Smilie's file.

'There's got to be something here,' I said, but nothing jumped out as we looked over the pages. There was nothing about Smilie being an alien.

'Her hobbies are listed as "theatre, yoga and ceroc".'

'I don't know what ceroc is but it doesn't sound particularly evil.'

'We just need to look more closely.' Jess was flicking through the pages. 'What were you expecting? Photos of her licking her lips over a brain on a plate?'

'Not exactly,' I said.

'A PhD in world domination?'

Now she was just taking the mickey. 'No.'

'A reference from Dr Evil?'

'Of course not!' I looked at the last page of Smilie's file. There was a long letter attached to the back which had the PALS logo at the top and was signed by someone called Montgomery McMonaghan.

'This looks interesting,' I said.

'Almost as interesting as finding a boy in the girls' toilets,' said a familiar voice that gave me the proper willies. 'Open the door and come out now,' she said, 'and don't try to hide the documents in your hand, I'll be taking those.'

We looked at each other. There was no escape.

The toilet door swung open and Jess and I squished out of the cubicle to where Miss Smilie was waiting with an especially annoying grin on her face. She snatched the papers out of my hand, glanced down at them and then put them into the inside pocket of her jacket. There was no way we were going to see those files again.

'So,' she said, tilting her head slightly in a way that made her look like an evil robot. 'Stealing confidential information from the school office: unarguably a punishable offence. You're coming with me to the PALS suite. Right now.'

She shoved us forward in front of her, towards the door.

I tried not to panic. I tried to come up with a plan, but I didn't see how we could argue our way out of it. How had she known we were in the office, and how did she know we were in the girls' toilets? It couldn't be a coincidence.

I pushed open the door and stepped into the corridor, almost bumping into Mrs Cobb and Mrs Halloway.

'Alex, dear, we've been looking for you. How are you feeling, poppet?' Mrs Halloway said.

'Oh, er, not good. I had to run to these toilets because I felt another gush coming on and they were the nearest.'

Mrs Cobb backed away.

'What's this?' Miss Smilie snapped.

'Thank goodness you found him, Miss Smilie.' Mrs Halloway bent down and put her hand on my forehead. 'Poor Alex is very unwell. I need to get him back to the medical room.'

'When I was in the toilets, I found Jess, and she's got it too,' I said, making the air stink and trying not to laugh at the disgusted expression on Jess's face.

'She does look a bit peaky,' Mrs Halloway said. 'Come on, you two, let's get you sat down with a glass of water.'

Miss Smilie's annoying, triumphant smile had changed into something quite different. She seemed to be deciding whether to argue with Mrs Halloway or not.

'Thank you, Miss Smilie, I'll take care of them, don't worry.' Mrs Halloway put her hands on our backs and started to push us gently back up the corridor.

'Well, I'll be sure to find you both later, to make sure you're taken care of,' Miss Smilie hissed.

I badly wanted to turn around and stick my tongue out at her, but sensed it would probably make things worse for us in the long run. It had been the squeakiest of close calls, but for a while, at least, we were safe.

We spent half of lunchtime in the medical room. Mrs Halloway phoned our mums, gave us some pink medicine that tasted of toothpaste and then left us on our own for some 'peace and quiet'.

'How did she know where we were?' Jess whispered. 'Everywhere we go she appears out of nowhere.'

'Do you think she injected us with tracking implants?'

'Don't you think we would have noticed if she injected us with tracking implants?'

'Maybe she put the implants in robotic bugs which crawled up our noses while we were asleep and now live under our skin.' I ran my hands down my arms. 'I think I can feel a lump.'

'Don't be so stupid!'

'Honestly, feel it, Jess.'

'I'm not feeling it.'

'Well, if there are tracking implants buried under our skin, I'll be happy to claw yours out for you.'

'And why didn't she tell Mrs Cobb and Mrs Halloway that she caught us with the staff files?'

'Staff file, you mean.'

'What?' Jess was in an especially bad mood and wasn't even attempting to be polite. I really don't know why I put up with her.

'She only took hers. I've still got Miss Fortress's.'

'That's something, I suppose. But why didn't she tell on us?'

'Think about it, Jess, if she told anyone we had her file, they'd want to know why. People would start asking questions. She clearly has as much to hide as we do.'

'So we were saved by the stink.'

'It's OK, you don't have to thank me,' I said.

'Wasn't going to.' She lay down on the little bed and cuddled up to the hot-water bottle Mrs Halloway had given her. She looked different like that, kind of small and sweet, like a baby squirrel. 'We really need to get out of here and get Bob.'

'Copy that.'

Fifteen minutes later, we finally convinced Mrs Halloway that we'd made a miraculous recovery and she released us from the medical room. I was almost sad to leave – it was so cosy in there, and it was nice to feel safe from Smilie and Fortress and the PALS army for a little while. But we were late collecting Bob; we'd left him for much longer than we'd intended.

We walked back to my classroom, and looked for Bob where we'd left him on a shelf behind a load of dusty science equipment.

'This is where we left him, right?' Jess called down from the table she was standing on.

'Yes, that's definitely the spot.' I had a horrible feeling spreading through my chest. 'Why?'

'He's not here.'

'He must be. Let me see, you're probably looking wrong.'

'How do you look wrong, Double-O-Divvy?'

I climbed up beside her and shoved all the stuff about on the shelf, making clouds of dust fly around us. It was pointless. Jess was right. Bob was gone.

The bell rang for afternoon registration, so Jess went back to her classroom and I sat at my desk, trying not to panic. I looked up as the door opened, expecting Miss Fortress to walk in, but the teacher who walked in was not Miss Fortress, it was Miss Smilie.

'For fluff's sake,' I said under my breath.

'Unfortunately, Miss Fortress has fallen ill and has had to go home,' Miss Smilie said.

'What's wrong with her, Miss?' one of the girls asked.

'Upset stomach, I believe.' Smilie looked at me. 'I've heard there's a nasty bug going around. I'll be taking your class this afternoon.'

I kept my head down for the rest of the day, not wanting to give her any excuse to march me off to the PALS suite. She didn't mention what had happened at lunch, but every time I looked up, she was watching me.

'Bob and Miss Fortress disappearing at the same time? That's too much of a coincidence,' Jess said as we were walking home.

'I know, it's weird. Something's definitely up with that. Our primary objective tomorrow morning is to locate Agent Bob.'

We turned onto Oak Avenue, which was a long street with trees all the way down both sides.

'I hope he's OK,' Jess said. 'You know how he hates surprises.'

'Wherever he is, he'll know we're coming for him. Agent Alex and She-Jerk never leave a man behind. We'll find out where he is and stage a daring rescue mission.'

'She-Jerk? SHE-JERK?'

'And what is up with Miss Smilie being everywhere we are?' I continued. 'There's no way she could have guessed we were hiding in the girls' toilets. It's the last place anyone would look for me.'

'I don't know,' Jess sighed.

'If you'd just have a feel of that lump…'

'Alex, there is not a tracking implant in your arm!' Jess shouted.

'Well, she's tracking us somehow.'

'If only we had that file. I'm sure we would have got some answers from it.'

'Who even has paper files, anyway?' I said. 'You don't see Ironman Tony Stark saving the world with a pile of A4 in his iron hand. It's so annoying and old personish. If it had been computer files, we could have copied them and hidden the memory stick. Smilie would never have caught us with them and we'd still have them now.'

'That's true,' Jess said, 'but Mrs Cobb looks after the staff files and she is *really* old.'

I sighed. 'Operation "Who's The Baddy?" – Current status: getting nowhere fast.'

As we reached the end of Oak Avenue, there

was a rustling noise in the tree behind us, and we turned to see a pigeon taking off from one of the branches.

'That looked like Dexter,' Jess said.

'How the heck can you tell? It was really high up. You're being paranoid.'

'But it looked like him.'

'Jess, if it was Dexter, he would have spoken to you. It was just a random pigeon. They all look the same.'

'Fine,' she huffed, 'but they don't all look the same. That's so offensive.'

We'd had a long, hard day and were both pretty grumpy, so we argued for the rest of the walk to my house. It was only when we were sat in the kitchen, trying to think of a good excuse to tell my mum about why Bob-slash-Miley was not in the tank that I suddenly remembered.

'Hey, I saw a name on it,' I said.

'A name on what?'

'That letter at the back of Smilie's file, the one with the PALS logo on it.'

'What name?'

'Erm, it was someone to do with PALS and it was a classic super-villain name.'

'What, exactly, is a classic super-villain name?'

'You know, first and last names start with the same letter and really tricky to spell. Morris Mackintosh ... Montessori McLachlan ... wait, I've almost got it ... Montgomery McMonaghan! That was it!'

'Montgomery McMonaghan?'

'Did you see that? I have a mind like a mega-pixel camera.'

'You remembered one name.'

'I know, I'm amazing.' Because, you know, I am.

'Let's Google it.'

I put my laptop on the kitchen counter and started to type the name into Google. It felt weird to be researching without Bob looking over our shoulders, pointing out our spelling mistakes. If I was Nick Fury of S.H.I.E.L.D., and Jess was Phil Coulson (from before he got stabbed through the heart by Loki, obvs), then Bob was definitely agent Maria Hill: far less significant but sometimes quite handy to have around.

I pressed enter, and Jess and I leaned closer to the screen.

A loud 'Boom!' from the laptop made us jump.

'Son of a biscuit!' I said. 'Are we under attack?'

'Worse,' said Jess, rolling her eyes. 'That was just a sound effect on the computer. Look!'

We watched the screen as the animated flames and smoke, which had appeared at the sound of the explosion, gradually disappeared to reveal a pop-up from The Professor.

'I guess that's his way of telling us he's angry,' Jess sighed. 'What a drama queen.'

'It was quite cool, though,' I smiled. 'You were super-scared, Jessticles. You should have seen your face!'

'I was too busy looking at you almost falling off your stool, Double-O-Chicken.'

'Nah, that name doesn't work. You need to stick with the alliteration.'

'Shut up and read.' Jess glared at me.

ALEX AND JESS
I GAVE YOU A SIMPLE TASK, WHICH
YOU HAVE FAILED TO COMPLETE.
NOW I HAVE A HEADACHE.

THIS IS UNACCEPTABLE!
FOCUS ON THE TASK I SET AND REPORT
BACK VIA PIGEON, OR I WILL BE FORCED
TO TAKE DRASTIC ACTION.
THE PROFESSOR

'Yeah, he seems a bit peed off,' I said.

'He seems a bit mad, you mean. How dare he threaten us?' Jess was furious. 'What's he going to do to us, anyway? Annoy us to death with his stupid pop-ups?'

'I don't know, Jess, he could be dangerous, with his pigeon assailants, his pop-up sorcery and his angry font.'

'Well, he doesn't scare me.'

'Yeah, same, same. I was just saying…'

At that moment, Jess's phone started ringing, and buzzing around on the counter in front of us. We both looked at it.

'OMG, it must be him!' I said.

'It's not him,' Jess said.

'But it says "No Caller ID". It's him, I tell you!'

'Now you're being a drama queen, Alex.'

'Answer it then,' I said, 'if you're not scared.'

We watched the phone vibrating like it was possessed by the devil. Jess's stupid rock music ringtone was ridiculously loud in my quiet kitchen.

'Probably just someone wanting me to claim my PPI or something,' Jess said.

'Yeah,' I said.

'But I'd better go home and make sure Mum doesn't answer the house phone.' Jess jumped up and buried her phone in the bottom of her bag.

'I think I'll unplug ours. You know, just in case.'

Jess ran out of the door and I ripped the phone cord out of the socket in the kitchen. I didn't fancy being electrocuted by a raging professor.

13

Into The Lipstick Lion's Lair

The next morning, I went to school with a lot on my mind. So much had happened over the past couple of weeks: not-so-superpowers; crazy kids; angry professors and talking goldfish, not to mention psycho Smilie and her tasting room. There was a lot to sort out, but our priority was Bob. The poor little guy was lost somewhere, alone and probably frightened. I'd told my mum that we were keeping him at school to study in science. She wasn't happy about it, and Lauren threw a right tantrum, but it was the best we could come up with. Whatever happened that day, we had to find him.

I tried to plan our next steps. Clearly Bob hadn't decided to double-cross us and roll himself away in his coffee jar. Somebody must have found him.

Miss Fortress walked into the room looking like she had the serious hump.

'I want whoever put the fish on the shelf to come and see me at break. I realise that you children have nothing better to occupy your minds than trying to exasperate me, but I refuse to be outwitted by a class of ten year olds.'

Most of the class looked confused, which was understandable really. What kind of prankster would put a fish on a shelf? Pretty lame prank. I tried to look confused too.

'Miss Fortress, do you mean a real fish?'

'Yes, a living, breathing goldfish, in a jar on the shelf, as one of you knows very well.'

She looked around, making eye contact with as many people as possible. She looked at me the longest. It was so unfair that I was the prime suspect. I know I did actually do it, but she had no way of knowing that. For some unknown reason, she'd recently decided to join the Anti Agent Alex Group, or as I liked to call it, 'Aaaaaaaagh'. So Miss Fortress had Bob. I always knew there was something fishy about her. Get it – *fishy*? I snorted at my own joke.

'Do you have something to say, Alex?' Miss Fortress glared at me.

At the risk of making her hate me even more, I had to find out what she had done with Bob.

'I like fish, Miss. Can we keep it as a class pet? We could call it Gregory.'

'Absolutely not.'

'But why, Miss? It would be a wonderful educational opportunity for us all. We could learn about, erm, fish stuff.'

Miss Fortress looked up at me. 'You seem very interested in this goldfish, Alex. Is there anything you'd like to tell me?'

'No, no, just crazy into goldfish right now.'

'How strange,' she said, 'I thought you'd devoted your life to superheroes.' She was definitely suspicious.

'Nah, Miss. Superheroes are over. It's all about goldfish, now. Am I right, guys?' I looked around the class, hoping for some back up, but they all just stared at me like they couldn't believe the new depths of lameness I'd plummeted to.

'The fish has been returned to the PALS aquarium where I assume it came from,' Miss Fortress said. 'And anyway, it didn't look like a Gregory.'

She opened her laptop and started to take the register.

Poor Bob.

When I filled Jess in at break, she was relieved to find out what had happened to Bob but agreed that we had to rescue him immediately, even though it meant going to the one place in school we were desperate to avoid.

At lunchtime, we waited around the corner from the PALS suite until we saw the kids filing out of the door before afternoon registration. We had two minutes to get in, get Bob and get back to our classrooms. It was going to be tighter than my mum's Zumba leggings. I started to edge into the corridor when Jess pulled me back.

'Someone's coming!' she hissed.

The door to the PALS suite was open and Jason

came walking out, looking very pleased with himself.

'That's odd,' I said. 'Why would Jason be in PALS? He loathes all that stuff.'

'Yeah, he doesn't seem like a love and hugs kind of boy. Watch out, he's coming this way!'

I looked around. In the movies, there's always a broom cupboard to hide in, but we had nothing. Just an empty corridor. We needed a plan B.

'Get the invisibility cloak!'

Jess sighed at me and grabbed my hand, just as Jason came around the corner.

'Scuzzo – what a surprise. I usually smell you coming from ten miles away. What are you doing hiding in the corridor with your freakish girlfriend?'

'None of your business,' Jess said, and made a big obvious fuss of letting go of my hand.

'Oh my God! You were holding hands! Were you two freaks kissing? This is brilliant, I can't wait to tell Ronnie.' He walked off, laughing.

'Was that necessary, Jess? Now they have another reason to make my life hell.'

'Seeing as your best idea was an invisibility cloak, I'd say it was necessary. And trust me, it was far more painful for me than it was for you. Now let's go, we're running out of time.'

We ran down the corridor, slipped inside the door and tiptoed into the main room, where Bob was being held captive.

'Do you have to do such a stupid exaggerated walk?' Jess snapped at me.

'Yes, I do. It makes the mission more fun. Have you heard about fun, Jess? Most people like to have it.'

'I have plenty of fun.'

'No, Jess, you're a fun-sucker. You suck the fun right out of everything.'

'Shut up, you're making too much noise. Someone will hear us.'

There was a loud click behind us as the door closed, and the sound of a key turning in the lock. I didn't dare turn around.

'She's right, someone will hear you, although Jessica's ridiculous boots were as loud as your attempts at whispering.'

Of course, Miss Smilie was behind us.

'I'm not even going to ask why you two are here, but I'm delighted that you've come. I've been wanting to get you into my suite for some time.'

For a few seconds we just stood there, saying nothing, trying to remember to breathe, while Miss Smilie smiled, not blinking, enjoying the fact that she finally had us in her clutches. For the first time I could remember, her smile looked genuine. It was a cold, cruel smile, and it didn't have the usual look of being forced onto her face, like it hurt her to have to stretch those muscles. It was spontaneous and it was real, and that scared me more than any of the threats-disguised-as-being-nice that she liked to dish out. I couldn't think of anything to say.

'We just wanted to look at the fish,' Jess said, with a face like my sister's when she's just been caught eating Nutella out of the jar with her finger. It wasn't the best excuse. Only Jess would make up stories to get herself out of trouble that are actually more truth than lies.

'If you join PALS, you can come and look at my fish as often as you like.'

Jess snorted. I suddenly felt a little less afraid.

'Come on, Miss, that's a terrible line! You're one step away from being a stranger trying to lure us into his van to see his puppies. There's a Life Coach play about that, just FYI.'

'Well, OMG don't you BFFs just make me LOL.'
She was getting annoyed.

'You shouldn't talk like that, Miss, it's not right for a woman of your age. Leave it for the kids or it's going to be embarrassing for all of us,' I said.

She took a few steps towards us, all casually, like she just wanted to have a chat about last week's *X-Factor*. Maybe I'd pushed her too far.

'I'm convinced that you're the perfect candidate for PALS, Alex. Why don't you come with me to the testing room, and we'll find out?'

'Oh! The *testing* room. Did you hear that, Jess? She wants us to go to the testing room.'

'Makes more sense.'

'Totally. I'd much rather be tested than tasted. Less brain eating, more spelling. I'm pretty good at spelling.'

'I don't think it's that kind of testing, Alex.' Jess was watching Smilie like a mouse watches a cat, which totally works because Jess is so small and Miss Smilie is all teeth and claws.

'Jessica is right. It's a short test to see if you're PALS material. And don't worry: everyone is PALS material, one way or another.'

Miss Smilie gave the door to the testing room

a gentle pull and it creaked open, loudly and slowly until we could see inside. In it was a single desk and chair. On the desk was a black box with some knobs and switches on it. It was blocky and had a few wires poking out of it – it looked like a games console from the olden days. Attached to it on a long, curly cord was a pair of huge headphones. I didn't know exactly what it was or how it worked, but I knew that if I put those headphones on, I'd never be the same again. Gulp.

'I told you your doors needed looking at, Miss. You should do something about that creak. You wouldn't want people thinking there was something sinister going on in there.'

'Why don't you step inside and put on the headphones?'

I can't tell you how much I didn't want to go in there. I was proper scared. I glanced over at the aquarium and locked eyes with Bob. He was swimming on the spot, just treading water, looking through the aquarium wall. I never would have thought that you could tell how a goldfish was feeling, just by looking at it, but I looked at Bob and I knew he was even more terrified than I was. I had to distract Smilie and buy some time for Jess to get him out.

'If you don't mind, I'd like to check out your equipment first. No offence, but it looks like you made it yourself and judging by your lack of proper door maintenance, I'd say that machine is a death trap.'

'No, Alex! Don't do it.' Jess grabbed my arm.

'I have to.' I nodded my head towards the aquarium so she would understand what I wanted her to do. She shook her head.

'Jess,' I said, 'sometimes you just have to YOLO it.'

I walked into the testing room.

'Take a seat, Mr Sparrow.' Miss Smilie had followed me in. The room was small so I was really close to her. She smelt like the cupboard where my mum keeps the safety pins and Calpol.

'Let me just do up my shoelace, I don't want to trip.' I started to bend down thinking I could unplug the machine without her noticing.

'Your shoes have velcro straps.'

'Oh, yes, my bad – I thought I was wearing my other shoes.' Why did my mum have to get me stupid velcro shoes? Clearly shoelaces were essential for spy work. I'd have to talk to her about it when I got home. If I got home. That was over-dramatic; I was obviously going to get home, even if I was talking in rhymes and forcing hugs on everyone.

'Now, let me take a look at this – maybe I can fix it for you? I got my sister's V-Tech working again after someone accidentally dropped it in the toilet.'

'Actually, we're getting an upgrade soon, and in the meantime this one works perfectly.'

She put a hand on my shoulder and pushed me down into the chair, sliding the testing machine away from me so it was just out of reach.

'Why are the walls all puffy?' I asked, trying to keep her talking so I could think up a brilliant plan.

'They're soundproofed, Alex. Once the door is closed, no one outside can hear what's happening inside. You could scream with all your might and nobody would ever know.'

OK, really wish I hadn't asked. I felt around in my pocket to see if there was anything in there that could help me. All I found was some Pokemon cards, an empty Haribo packet and a mini can of air freshener I'd started carrying around with me, for obvious reasons.

I had an idea.

'I think I can smell that unpleasant odour you mentioned before, Miss.' I sniffed the air, which obviously ponged because, hey, I was in the room and I'd told a couple of lies.

Miss Smilie sniffed too. 'Yes, that stench does seem to follow you around, but we won't need to worry about that any longer.' She picked up the headphones.

'I'm just going to freshen the room up a bit,' I said, and I sprayed the air freshener in Smilie's direction.

She breathed a bit in and started to cough.

'Woah, the stink is so bad, it's making you choke! I'd better spray some more.' I jumped out of the chair, spraying as I backed towards the door and got out into the main room at the same time as Jess came running towards me with her bag. At that moment, Miss Fortress came in through the double doors. We were trapped. Miss Smilie was striding out of the testing room, and Miss Fortress barred our escape.

'Hope,' Miss Smilie smiled, 'what are you doing

here? I was just inducting these two pupils into the PALS scheme.'

'Oh, I thought the suite was empty! We were discussing the study of fish in class earlier, so I came to have a look at your wonderful aquarium. Mr Crumpet let me in. I hope you don't mind, Joanna.' Miss Fortress looked at Jess and me. 'I'm sure Alex and Jess would benefit from a bit of calming meditation. Amongst other things. But what is that dreadful smell? It doesn't seem conducive to peace and mindfulness.'

'Mr Sparrow detected an odour problem and was trying to eradicate it. I was just about to help him get rid of it … permanently.'

'Then let me help you!' Miss Fortress snatched the can of air freshener out of my hand and started waving it around, spraying and spraying. The smell filled the room in a lemon-scented fog. It was so strong that it made my eyes water. It was so strong that I could taste it. Miss Fortress was clearly as keen to get rid of my stink as everyone else was.

With both Fortress and Smilie there, I didn't know how we were going to get away.

That's when the fire alarm went off.

'Oh no! I must have sprayed too close to the smoke detectors!' Miss Fortress said, tossing the empty can across the room into the bin. 'Alex, Jess, you'd better leave by the fire exit and join your classes at the congregation point on the field. I'll go and explain to the Head.'

She held the door open for us and we ran.

When we got outside, panting for breath, Jess turned to me and said, 'Alex, are you OK?'

'Yes, friend!' I gave her my best PALS smile. It was mean, I know, but I couldn't help myself.

'No! Alex, I'm so sorry, I shouldn't have let you go in there.' Jess looked like she was going to cry. 'What am I going to do now?'

'Tell me you got Bob out OK.' I grinned at her.

She punched me hard in the arm. 'So not funny, Alex.'

'You should have seen your face, though!'

'I hate you.'

'Nah, you don't. Judging by how upset you were when you thought I'd become a PALS pal, I'd say you actually like me. Loads.'

'Only because I felt responsible for you in the same way I would if a stray cat turned up at my door.'

'You're saying these words, but all I can hear is, "I love you, Alex!"'

'I'm never talking to you again.'

We were almost at the fire drill congregation point on the field and had to separate to join our classes. I waved at Darth, who was waiting for Jess.

'Did you get Bob?'

'Yeah, I got him. He's in one piece but I think he's in shock. We need to get him home.'

'Meet you at the gate after school?'

'See you there.'

We walked home from school super-fast, raced to Bob's tank and gently tipped him in.

'How did Smilie know we were there again?' I said. 'She must have a marauder's map.'

'She has not got a marauder's map,' Jess huffed. 'But I do think she has something which is telling her where we are.'

'Well, whatever it is, we need to get rid of it. We can't get away with anything anymore.' I was so hot from all that running around that I had to take my hat off.

'Please put that back on, Alex,' Jess said. 'I could

really do without having to deal with the full horror of your ear this evening.'

'That's rude.'

'With your ear and that awful air freshener, I've already thrown up in my mouth today.'

She picked up my hat and raised her arm as if she was going to throw it at me. But she stopped.

'Weird,' she said.

'Yes. Yes you are.'

'No, not me. Your hat.'

'I thought you liked my hat!'

'I do! But I can feel something inside it.'

'What do you mean?' I said, and I snatched it out of her hand. 'Oh, fudge, you're right, there is something in there. Maybe it's a spider.'

I dropped it on the floor.

'I don't think it's a spider,' Jess said, looking down at it.

'How can you be sure, though?' I asked, climbing onto one of the high stools at the breakfast bar, just in case.

'It would have run off when you dropped it. Or at least I would have heard it swear when it hit the floor. Poor thing.'

'Oops, yeah,' I said. 'Sorry, mister not-there

spider. It's just, with your fat body and long legs, and the running and stuff, you freak me out.'

'Alex, you're talking to a not-spider. That's a new low, even for you.'

'But if it's not a spider, then what is it and how did it get there?'

'Someone must have put it there,' Jess said. 'Can you think when that might have happened?'

'No!' I said, horrified. 'It's always on my head!'

We stood in silence, looking at my hat like it was a pile of dog poo on the kitchen floor. And then, I remembered.

'Except for the time Smilie caught me at the PALS door and told me to take it off. I put it in my pocket, though.'

'Are you sure?'

'I think so, but I rushed off.'

'And when did you next have it after that?'

'We were in the playground, practising the adamantium filter and Jason found it on the floor...'

I trailed off as I realised what had happened.

'You must have dropped it at the PALS suite,' Jess said. 'Then Smilie must have taken it and planted it in the playground.'

'What's she done to it, Jess?' I whispered.

'We need to check it out,' she said. 'You'd better pick it up.'

'Why don't you pick it up?' I said, not wanting to touch it.

'It's your hat.'

'Fine!' I rolled up a magazine that was on the kitchen counter and poked at the hat with it. Nothing happened.

'What do you think it's going to do? Explode?'

Yes. 'No, of course not.'

Jess raised an eyebrow. 'Alex, you've been wearing it for days. If she'd wanted to blow you up, she'd have done it by now.'

I braced myself, bent down and picked it up. I shook it and turned it inside out but couldn't see anything unusual.

'Try under the forehead flap,' Jess said.

I lifted the furry flap and gasped. Hidden underneath was a tiny, black, metal device.

'What the hell is that?' Jess backed away.

'I've seen these before,' I said, with the air of an experienced agent. 'Tracking device.'

'What? Where have you seen them before?'

'At the Aaaaaaaaaah. And on TV.'

'So that's how she turns up everywhere we are. How awful!'

I ripped the device out of my poor hat and threw it on the floor. 'This evil must be destroyed,' I said in my best Batman voice, and I lifted my foot to stomp on it.

'Wait!' Jess shouted.

'Why? We need to get rid of it! She knows where we are ALL THE TIME!'

'Yes, but she doesn't know that we know that she knows. We could use this.'

I put my foot back down. It was quite good thinking from Jess, though I wasn't about to tell her that. 'So we keep it and pretend we haven't found it?'

'Exactly. At least for a while.'

'OK, but I'm putting it at the bottom of the drawer for now. I don't want to look at it.'

'Me neither,' Jess said. 'Let's see what Bob found out.'

The poor little guy was still a bit shaky. Before we asked him about the mission, we let him talk for a while about his time in the PALS aquarium. You have to understand that for a dude who needs everything to be exactly a certain way, being in a new environment with a hundred strange fish was a nightmare. They kept trying to talk to him; they kept swimming in places where someone else had just pooed; they invaded his personal space. He said he would have died if it hadn't been for one gentle, kind and symmetrically pleasing fish called Elle, who found him a quiet corner and kept the others away.

'So, what the beep happened in there? I was in the testing room and when I ran out, Miss Fortress was suddenly there, acting like a maniac as usual. Why did she come? Her looking at the fish excuse was weak. Was she trying to help Smilie?'

'I'm not sure,' Jess said. 'I would say they don't like each other from the way they were talking.'

'What do you mean? They were all, "Hello, Hope", "Hello, Joanna". They seemed pretty friendly to me.'

'You know nothing about girls, Alex Sparrow. When girls are overly polite like that it usually means they hate each other.'

'Girls are weird.'

'Not as weird as you.'

We had Miss Fortress's staff file laid out on the

breakfast bar but there was nothing useful in it. The whole day had been a disaster. We'd taken so many risks, all for nothing.

'Bob, what happened when you were spying on Miss Fortress? Did you see anything to suggest that she's an evil psychopath?'

Jess began to twitch. 'He said she mostly sat at her computer, eating a Chunky Kit-Kat. At one point she got up and went over to one of the windows. She leaned out and was talking to someone, but he couldn't see who it was.'

'Could he hear what she said?'

'She spoke very quietly, and he could only see her profile so it was difficult to lip-read. He couldn't really make any of it out. When she turned away from the window, she spotted him, huffed about a lot and then took him to the PALS room.'

'Well that's all a bit weird again, but there's still nothing definite. How will we ever know which side Miss Fortress is on?'

'Another dead end,' Jess said. 'Let's Google that Montgomery McMonaghan guy – we forgot last night.'

'Yeah, we were distracted by the pop-up of doom.'

I grabbed my laptop from upstairs and put it on the counter, then went to get some snacks while Jess typed the name into Google.

'It says he's the head of a corporation called SPARC,' she said.

'That is the perfect super-villain job,' I said, all excited. 'What does the company do?'

'It's all stuff to do with fitness, health and wellbeing. Apparently SPARC stands for Strength, Peace, Activity, Recreation and Clarity.'

'Sounds like PALS.'

'It does sound like PALS,' Jess agreed.

'Do you think they're connected?' I asked.

But Jess had started twitching away, apparently having a conversation with Bob.

'What now?' I said, annoyed that he'd stolen my moment.

'He says he's thought of something else that might help us.'

'Really? What is it?'

'He'll only tell us if we agree to play Scrabble with him once a week.'

'For how long?'

'Forever.'

I saw our evenings stretching out ahead of us,

being beaten at word games by a goldfish when we could have been doing something fun. Unfortunately, we were desperate and Bob knew it. 'Fine, but it had better be good.'

When Jess stopped twitching she turned and looked at me, mouth wide open.

'Oh, my God.'

'What?'

'I can't believe we didn't think of it before.'

'What?'

'We're idiots.'

'Tell me!'

'If you rearrange the letters of her name: Hope Fortress is an anagram of The Professor!'

14

Jess vs Fortress

'How did you figure it out?' Miss Fortress looked up from her computer. She didn't try to deny it. She didn't even seem very surprised.

Jess and I had agreed not to give anything away, so I put on my best smooth-operative-under-interrogation voice: 'It wasn't so hard.'

'I slipped up. I lied in class. But I didn't think that would be enough for you to guess who I was.'

'It was enough to make us suspicious and we worked the rest out later.' Jess had that look on her face again. She was really good at doing hostile.

'And Miss, the whole name-anagram thing dropped you right in it.'

'Ah, yes, I couldn't resist that. I thought it was ever so clever. Didn't you think it was brilliant? And I really didn't think anyone would work it out.'

'So you underestimated us,' I said.

'Apparently so.'

We stood for a moment, sizing each other up. Miss Fortress looked pretty hacked off. Jess looked like someone had just threatened to confiscate her entire supply of studded bracelets. I stood between them, thinking hard about what to do next.

'We want some answers,' I said.

'I'll answer your questions if you answer mine.'

'OK, we'll start,' Jess said. She could be quite intimidating when she wanted to be. 'Who are you? I mean really?'

'I'm just a scientist. By day I teach under the name of Hope Fortress and by night I carry out research in the lab.'

'So you're an actual professor?' I couldn't quite take it in.

'Yes. Why? Were you expecting Albert Einstein?'

Yes.

'Sorry to disappoint you but having mad hair and a moustache isn't a prerequisite for being a professor. My turn: what have you found out about what's going on at the school?'

'We've found out that kids are being brainwashed,' Jess said. 'We've found out that Miss Smilie is evil. We've found out that you aren't who we thought you were, so how can we trust you?'

Miss Fortress lit up. 'I knew Joanna Smilie was behind it. No normal person smiles that much! And that PALS nonsense – all those ridiculous affirmations. I'm almost relieved that it's a cover for a diabolical scheme.'

Jess and I looked at each other. Perhaps Miss Fortress could be trusted.

We gave her a quick rundown of what we'd learnt – it was the only way we were going to get the answers we wanted. She listened and nodded and I got the feeling she was on our side. Jess was still angry and suspicious though, especially when she found out that Dexter had been spying on us with a recording device strapped to his leg. Do you remember that scratching I heard when we broke into the office? That was Dexter at the window. And that time we saw a pigeon in Oak Avenue? Yep, him again.

Once we'd filled her in, it was time for Miss Fortress to explain what the heck was going on.

'The intricacies of brain function are a mystery. I have devoted my life to finding out how to access inactive areas of the brain and unleash their potential. Some years ago, during our experiments, my lab partner and I stumbled upon a process that allowed us to inhibit brain function. Fearing that our discovery might be used for evil means, I took my research and fled from the organisation that employed me. I left everything behind and changed my identity.'

'In English, Miss?'

'But I've been working on this speech for ages, so that in the event you found me out, I'd have a compelling and dramatic monologue.'

'You probably need to get over yourself then, Miss. I'm ten. Jess is eleven. All we're hearing is fancy blah blah blahs.'

'How annoying. Fine. I was working as a scientist for an organisation when my partner and I discovered a way to control minds. I thought they might use our knowledge to do bad stuff so I suggested that my lab partner and I should leave and keep our techniques to ourselves. But he plotted against me. He used the research to move up the ranks and planned to get rid of me. When I found out, I ran away and changed my identity. I took all my notes and files but I knew there was a chance they'd have enough information to be able to do the mind-controlling without me. I kept an eye on the organisation and sure enough, I found out they had plans involving your school.'

'So you came here, tricked us into buying powers and sent us to do your dirty work for you while you hid away?' Jess was obviously not about to forgive The Professor that easily.

'I wouldn't have put it that way…'

'No, you would have put it in another, much longer, more boring way, because apparently you really love the sound of your own voice.'

Woah, I'd never seen Jess this angry.

'Jess,' I whispered, 'she's still a teacher, remember, she can keep us in at break if she wants to.'

'I don't care. She lost my respect when she decided to use pop-ups and a pigeon to pass on her orders, rather than asking us to our faces.'

She turned back to Miss Fortress. 'Do you know how much danger we've been in? Do you have any idea how hard it's been for us? Especially Alex. You can't give someone like him a superpower and just leave him to get on with it. He got himself in a right mess.'

'Yeah … I mean, hey!' A bit harsh, Jess.

Miss Fortress looked kind of guilty. 'I did try to guide you both. I got you together, I stepped in when I realised you might be in trouble.'

'She did do that, Jess. She did help us yesterday.'

'What were you doing in the PALS suite, anyway?' Jess was not going to let this go.

'Dexter recorded you talking about some kind of rescue, and then you seemed strangely interested in that goldfish. I used my advanced powers of deduction to work out where you'd be. And lucky for you both that I did!'

'So we're supposed to be grateful? You made me twitch and you made him stink. You ruined his life!'

'Ah, the side effects,' she said. 'I am sorry about those. There's no way of predicting exactly how they'll manifest themselves. Different every time.'

'So you knew there was a chance of it happening?'

'I suppose I did, yes.'

'We should report you to the NSPCC.'

'I thought some minor side effects would be a small price to pay for superhuman powers.'

Jess was fuming. 'What do you mean, "small price"? We paid nineteen ninety-nine for these powers and it really wasn't clear exactly what we were buying when we clicked the mouse.'

'It was all in the terms and conditions. You should always read the terms and conditions. Let that be a lesson to you.'

Jess launched herself at Miss Fortress and I'm not sure what would have happened if I hadn't pulled her back. For a small person, she was pretty strong. Perhaps Tiny Terror was the right sidekick name for her after all.

'Ladies! Let's just chillax a bit, shall we? We're not getting anywhere with you two scrapping like Han and Leia in *Star Wars*. Oh no wait, they end up kissing, that's a bit weird – forget I said that.'

They both looked at me like I was a complete moron.

'That's more like it. Now let's back up a bit. I want to know how you gave us our powers. Is it that mind-control business you were talking about?'

'Not exactly. The process can be used in two ways, though my old organisation only knows how to achieve one of them: the capacity to freeze areas of the brain. From what you've told me, I suspect that Miss Smilie is using the freezing procedure to control the children at Cherry Tree Lane. The process I used on you is the reverse: it stimulates areas of the brain to give a person enhanced abilities. I developed this process alone and have never revealed it to anybody, for fear of it being misused.'

'Still not quite with you…'

'OK, imagine that every child in the world is a muffin. There are infinite possibilities for flavour combinations – toffee and banana, pecan and apricot, carrot and courgette. Anything is possible and every muffin is different…'

'I think I'm triple chocolate: dark and delicious with delightful surprises inside.'

Jess made a rather disrespectful noise that sounded like a snigger.

'Shut up, Jessticles. What would you be? A Tesco Value muffin that's been dropped on the floor and put on the whoopsie shelf for 2p.'

'Better that than a delusional boy who thinks

he's a chocolate muffin and uses phrases like "whoopsie shelf".

'Excuse me!' Miss Fortress interrupted us. 'Please stop bickering and pay attention! As I was saying, what the Neuro-Electric Impulse Transmutation Procedure…'

'The what?'

'She means the spark-in-the-ear thing, dunce-boy.'

'Oh, the sparking, I get you. Sorry, carry on.'

'One of the things the Neuro-Electric Impulse Transmutation Procedure does is to stimulate areas of the brain. This is the procedure that you two have undergone. So you are still your own unique muffin but with a special ingredient added, like chocolate sprinkles on top.'

'Nice.'

'But the reverse procedure does something different. It freezes areas of the brain, like the part that makes people naughty or challenging which effectively makes each muffin revert back to the basic batter. The "cook" – in this case Miss Smilie – can then add whatever ingredients she likes to the batter, let's say it's blueberries…'

'Why blueberries?'

'Because blueberry muffins are boring,' Jess huffed at me. 'Pipe down, Sparrow.'

'What's your beef with blueberries, Prof? I can call you Prof, can't I?'

'Certainly not, and I have no beef with blueberries, I'm just using them for an example.'

'But I quite like blueberry muffins.'

'Shut up Double-O-Dumby. She's trying to explain.'

'Anyway, in this way, Miss Smilie, using those headphones in the testing room, can turn every child into the same muffin. Imagine a whole world of blueberry muffins. Every child a blueberry muffin. Nothing but blueberry muffins.'

'Hold up,' I said, 'how is Smilie adding the blueberries?'

'There are various ways. Think about how the brain takes in information – through reading, watching television…'

'The PALS videos!' I said.

'And that awful music Smilie plays!' Jess added.

'But even though the PALS stuff is the boringest rubbish ever, it doesn't seem like it's feeding us any information. It's just pictures of dolphins and feelings. How is it making those kids act like nutjobs?'

'That's what I need you two to find out.'

'So what you're saying is that you gave Jess and me chocolate sprinkles so that we can find some way of stopping Miss Smilie from sparking every kid at school and blueberry muffining them?'

'Yes, that's about it.'

Blimey.

'Why couldn't you just do it yourself?' Jess said.

'I can't break my cover,' Miss Fortress said. 'You can't imagine how bad things would get if he discovered me.'

'Is that really likely, Miss?' I said. 'No offence but he's just a scientist – what's he going to do? Flap his lab coat at you? How dangerous can he be?'

'He's a very powerful man now with hundreds of people working for him. He has unlimited resources and spies everywhere. He couldn't *be* more dangerous. And frankly, I find your attitude to scientists extremely offensive.'

'Fine,' Jess interrupted. 'You were too scared to investigate yourself, so you tricked a couple of kids into doing it.'

'But why did you choose us?' I said. 'I mean I can understand why you chose me; I've got skills, but Jess? Why her?'

'Yeah, you've got skills in hacking people off and coming up with rubbish ideas.'

'Shush, little Jessticles – back in your box.'

Fortress was looking from me to Jess. She seemed a bit alarmed. Anyone would think she was regretting her choice of super-helpers. 'Both of you were chosen because of your superior qualities. Alex, you have an extremely high IQ and a remarkable knack of being able to think on your feet. Jess, I chose you because you are sensible…'

'You mean boring, Miss,' I said.

'No, I mean that Jess has common sense – something which you are lacking, Alex. Jess also has a fierce sense of right and wrong, is honest and fearless. And she has really nice hair.'

'Er, what's wrong with my hair?'

'Your hair's fine.'

'Fine? That means rubbish.'

'No, it means it's fine. Pleasant … inoffensive.'

'Ha ha,' Jess said. 'Alex has got the hair version of, like, Captain America.'

'I do not have Captain America hair. I'm dark and edgy. My hair's a hundred per cent Hulk!'

'Only in your head, Cap.'

'But I don't want to be the boringest Avenger.'

'Too late. The Professor said so.'

Miss Fortress put her hands on her hips. 'Do you two do this all the time? I'm surprised you manage to get anything done.'

'We get loads done, no thanks to you.' Jess was back on the attack. 'You should have a bit of respect – you chose us because we were superior, remember?'

'Only in comparison to the rest of your school. It's not like I had the choice of every child in the nation.'

The conversation went on like that for quite a long time. Just my luck to get stuck with the two most argumentative women in the world. Naturally, as I have an extremely high IQ, I came out on top, but not until Jess had picked off most of her nail varnish and Miss Fortress had drunk about five cups of coffee. At least I think it was coffee.

And then I remembered the tracker. I pulled it out of my pocket and showed it to Miss Fortress.

'Is this a tracking device, Miss?'

'It looks like it,' she said, picking it up and examining it. 'Although there's some residue on it which is probably stopping it from working as well as it should. Where did you get it?'

'Miss Smilie planted it in my hat,' I said.

Miss Fortress did a girly scream and dropped it on the floor.

'I knew there was something wrong with that hat,' she said. 'Other than the obvious.'

'Hey!' I said. 'Is that why Dexter pooed on it? To try to help us? I thought it was because he hated me.'

'He does hate you,' said Miss Fortress. 'But his faeces helped disable the device. As far as I'm concerned you've scraped through, so far, thanks to my assistance and blind luck.'

'Well, as far as I'm concerned,' Jess said, 'you've scraped through, so far, thanks to our assistance, which you obtained through trickery and lies. Give me one good reason why I shouldn't expose you on my vlog.'

Miss Fortress turned on Jess. 'Everything I've done has been for a cause far greater than you, or me, or even this school. Why did you bring this tracker here? You've put me in grave danger!' She lifted her foot to stomp on the tracker.

'No!' I shouted.

'But we need to destroy it. As long as it functions, Joanna Smilie knows exactly where you are all the time.'

'Yes,' I said. 'But she doesn't know that we know that she knows.'

'Good thinking, Alex,' Miss Fortress said. 'Perhaps I *was* right to choose you.'

Jess glared at both of us.

'You two should go – the bell's going to ring in five minutes and I need a coffee before registration,' Miss Fortress said, opening the door and scanning the corridor. 'Make sure no one sees you and don't bring that ghastly tracker back in here, except during class.'

She pushed us out of the classroom and closed the door.

'Nice talking to you, too,' Jess stormed down the corridor not especially quietly. Apparently she was still mad.

'Chill out, Jessticles, we should be celebrating.'

'Celebrating the fact that we've been experimented on by a scientist on the run who has disguised herself as a teacher so she can watch us without our knowledge and then send us into danger on her behalf?' Definitely still mad.

'You're looking at it all wrong, as usual,' I said. 'Using their incredible superpowers and first-class spying skills, Agent Alex and The Frowner have discovered the identity of The Professor...'

'Please stop,' Jess sighed.

'With the help of their mysterious ally, they have uncovered a plot to shock their classmates into submission...'

'Shut up.'

'And only they can stop it. They are the heroes. They are the chosen ones.'

'At least we know how our powers work now, I suppose,' Jess said, as she walked down the steps to the playground.

It was only then that I realised: I'd forgotten to ask The Professor if she could take mine away.

15

I Become A PAL

It was getting harder to practise controlling my power in the playground. Where there used to be kids bombing around playing tag and arguing over who was It, now there were groups of children talking quietly or reading PALS books. We had no idea how many kids had been blueberried, but there seemed to be more every day. Knowing exactly who was a PAL wasn't easy. Even the kids who hadn't been changed were acting differently because everyone was afraid of doing something that might get them sent to the PALS suite. Nobody shouted. Nobody ran. Lots of people smiled, but nobody laughed.

Jess and I were discussing our next move when Dexter flew down to join us.

'Is it a message from Miss Fortress?' I asked Jess when she stopped twitching.

'Yes. She said to get to the side gate, fast – there's something going on she wants us to investigate.'

We hid the tracking device by the Friendship Bench and then walked as fast as we could without drawing attention to ourselves. Now that we knew exactly what Miss Smilie was doing to the kids, we were especially keen not to do anything that might get us into trouble. The thought of being controlled by her made me feel sick.

When we got close enough to see the gate, we hid behind one of the big cherry trees that grow down that side of the school. Miss Smilie stood waiting at the side of the building. She was dressed in dark reddy-purple; the same colour as the rotten cherries which had fallen from the trees and were squashed all over the ground. She had a matching smile, which stretched slowly across her face as a delivery truck pulled up.

Miss Smilie was at the driver's door before he even had a chance to get out. He handed her a clipboard with some paperwork on it and she backed off a few paces to read it as the driver got out of the truck and opened the back doors.

'What's she saying to him?' Jess asked.

'How do I know? My ear lie-detects, it doesn't pick up conversations from a hundred miles away. I might be able to lip-read but I can't see through that blonde mess you call hair.' It was frustrating, but I couldn't see a way of getting close enough to hear.

The driver brought a large cardboard box to Miss Smilie and put it on the floor in front of her. She barked something at him, and he went back to the front of his truck, got something out and handed it to her, looking very much like he wished he could get back in his truck and drive away.

'What did he give her?' I asked Jess.

'Not sure.'

'Oh my God, it's a knife! She's probably going to use it to cut his brain out, or…'

'…open that box. You're such a drama queen, Alex.'

Miss Smilie opened the box, looked inside and full-on Joker grinned. She signed the paperwork, turned to the open door behind her and nodded. A procession of blueberry kids marched out and started picking up the boxes that the driver had unloaded and carrying them into the school.

'We need to see what's inside those boxes. Whatever it is, it made Smilie super happy, and that can't be a good thing,' I said. 'It has to be something to do with PALS! But how are we going to get close enough without her seeing us?'

'I'll ask Dexter,' Jess said.

Dexter took off and swooped over to the gate, getting so close that he almost collided with Miss Smilie.

'He'll never make a good agent if that's his way of sneaking. He's so obvious!' I snorted.

'He's a pigeon, Agent Airhead, he can be as obvious as he likes; it's not as if she's going to suspect him.' Jess pushed me back behind the tree so she could get the best view.

Dexter swooped past Smilie again. She swatted at him with the clipboard but he flew up so he was just out of reach and perched on a ledge above the doorway.

'It's almost as if he's trying to wind her up,' I said.

'Yeah,' Jess said, 'Dexter knows exactly what he's doing.'

We both chuckled.

When Dexter returned, he described to Jess what he had seen.

'The boxes are stamped with the PALS logo,' Jess said, 'and inside are lots of smaller boxes, all the same, with pictures of mini devices like the ones we use for listening to music. At least I think that's what Dexter said.'

'That means earphones. That can't be good.'

'There are dozens of boxes – there must be a thousand devices inside. Do you think they can all do what the machine in the testing room does? Miss Smilie did say she was getting an upgrade.'

'We need to find out.'

'We need to get hold of one of those devices.'

'We need a diversion!'

I tried to think of something that would get Smilie away from the boxes without us getting into trouble, but before I could even mention the words 'ninjas' and 'laughing gas', Dexter took off. As he swooped past the school, he dropped the most enormous poo all over Smilie, who looked completely disgusted. She shouted and threw the clipboard at him, but he dodged it and made a strange cooing noise, which I'm pretty sure was a pigeon laugh. Miss Smilie disappeared back into the school, taking the open box with her.

'Now's our chance,' Jess said.

'We still need to get past the blueberries without looking like we're doing anything naughty. If they see us taking a box, they'll report us to Smilie. Remember what happened to The Sniffler?'

'I assume you've come up with a genius plan?'

'As it happens, Jessticles, I have, and it involves one of my favourite things: going undercover. You stay here, I can't have you blowing it all with your inability to do anything even slightly dishonest.'

'Hold on, hadn't we better think it through first?'

'There's no time. I'm going in.'

My plan was simple. To get in amongst the PALS, I had to be a PAL: walk like a PAL, talk like a PAL, smile like a PAL. The hardest part was going to be making sure my lie detector didn't go off. If the PALS pals smelled my stink, they would know I was less blueberry flavoured and more scummy toilet flavoured, and the mission would fail.

I smoothed down my uniform, straightened my back, lifted my chin and walked towards them. Yeah, it was hard to walk without my usual swag, but a good agent has to be able to adapt himself to any situation.

As I got close, I pulled out the PALS smile. The PALS smile is different from a normal person's smile, and also different from Miss Smilie's I-want-to-murder-you smile. The PALS smile is the most innocent, carefree, joyful and slightly moronic smile you will ever see. To get it right, I had to think the way a PAL would think: freshly made beds, a healthy salad, everything in alphabetical order...

'Hello, friend!' I said to the pupil formerly known as Pushatron. 'I've come to assist you with these boxes.'

'Hello to you, friend! There are many boxes – an extra pair of hands would be PALStastic! Did Miss Smilie send you?'

Here goes… 'Yes, friend! She said, "It's so much better to share the work than to sit and watch Miley Cyrus twerk."' I know, I know, but it was the best I could come up with on the spot.

Pushie's smile flickered. 'I don't know that affirmation. How strange, I thought I knew them all.'

'It's from a rare, limited-edition PALS book; hard to find in mint condition but it has affirmations *for days*. Miss Smilie has a copy, obvs, because she's just so wonderful!'

I waited for the buzz, followed by the stink, followed by Pushatron running off screaming to Miss Smilie, but finally my adamantium wall seemed to be working. The fart didn't come. Yesssss!

'Miss Smilie is the most wonderful teacher and guide!' P-tronny was beaming again. 'Thank you, friend! Grab a box!'

I picked up a box and started walking towards the PALS suite, feeling pretty smug that my genius plan had worked. Then I realised that the box was sealed and I had no way of getting one of the devices out without it being really obvious. I stared hard at the box, hoping I could use the force to open a small hole, pull one out, and then reseal the hole. It didn't work. I didn't panic, because a good agent always keeps his head. Instead I ran to the classroom that was closest to where Jess was hiding in the playground.

I opened the window and used a special Secret Agent code to get Jess's attention. She made sure the coast was clear and then ran to the window.

'Why are you waving at me like a maniac?' Jess asked.

'I ran into an unforeseen problem,' I said.

'You mean because you didn't think the plan through?'

'No.'

'Really?'

'Fine, Jessticles, if that's what you want to hear. But just so you know, there's nothing wrong with a bit of YOLO. If I didn't YOLO sometimes, we'd never get anything done.'

'What's the problem, dufus?'

'It's...'

'No, wait – let me guess... You don't know how to get a device out of the box without making it look obvious.'

Right. Exactly right. SO ANNOYING! 'I have a

plan – we need a lightsaber, a memory eraser and a hamster.'

'We need a puddle and some keys.'

'What?'

'Give me the box, Alex,' Jess sighed.

I passed the box out of the window. Jess dropped it in a puddle, waited a minute and then tore a hole in one of the soggy corners using her keys. Because it was wet, the cardboard ripped easily, and it looked like the hole had been caused by some random accident. I was impressed.

'Don't think this is going to make me reconsider your sidekick status,' I said, as she handed the box back to me. I pulled a device through the hole as I ran back out of the classroom and down the corridor. I ditched the box at the bottom of the pile outside the PALS suite and then legged it back to the Friendship Bench.

'Told you my plan would work,' I said.

Classic Jess eye-roll.

'Let's have a look at Smilie's new toy.'

The device was just as Dexter had described it: a tiny, metal, pebble-shaped electronic machine with a touchscreen and earphones attached. It looked beast, actually; much sleeker and more high-tech than my battered old iPod shuffle. Beneath the screen was the PALS logo, and 'PALpod' in shiny writing.

'That's some upgrade,' Jess said. 'These must have cost loads to get made. I wonder where she's getting all the money from?'

'Maybe that Montgomery McMonaghan guy.'

We sat in silence and inspected it, sitting innocently in the palm of my hand. I think we could both guess what it was for, but there was only one way to be sure.

'Why don't you turn it on so we can see exactly what it does?' I said in the voice version of sidling.

'No chance. You do it.'

'We both know that as the lead agent, I'm too important to risk. Turning on the evil brainwashing device is definitely more of a job for a sidekick.'

'Good thing I'm not a sidekick, then.'

'If you're not a sidekick, why do they call you The Shaking Dwarf?'

'They don't, Double-O-Delusional.'

'Well, if I'm too valuable to turn it on, and you're too scared to turn it on, who can we get to turn it on?'

We looked at each other as the idea came to us at the same moment.

'Miss Fortress!'

16

Mufti Mayhem

Mufti Day: some call it non-uniform; some call it dress-down (though TBH, not wearing your school uniform is definitely a step up, not down). We call it mufti. It's a day of freedom; a day of joy; a day that provides an insight into the non-uniformed lives of every kid at school; a day that separates the super-cool from the geeks and freaks. There's a lot of pressure to choose the right outfit – one bad decision and you'll be laughed at until the next Mufti Day. And of course there is the ultimate shame: being The Kid Whose Mum Forgot It Was Mufti Day And Came To School In School Uniform.

I was so excited about Mufti Day that I almost forgot about all the bad stuff that was happening. We'd given the PALpod to Miss Fortress to investigate and were waiting to hear what she'd discovered. In the meantime, I thought I'd earned the chance for a little relax. I'd planned to meet Jess and Darth Daver at the gate, though they probably wouldn't recognise me because I looked so gangster. There was no chance of not recognising those two: DD in his usual head-to-toe black, long sleeves pulled down over his hands so just the tips of his fingers showed; and Jess in skinny jeans, pretend leather jacket (apparently wearing real leather is 'loathsome and vile and evil and cruel') and her usual massive boots.

'Hey, guys, it's me!'

'OMG, really? But you look so edgy! I totally thought you were someone else.'

Bums to Jess – she always makes me question myself. Things I thought I absolutely, definitely knew, I'm suddenly not so sure of.

'Are you saying there's something wrong with my clothes?'

'There's nothing wrong with your clothes, if you want to look like Harry Potter on his day off.'

'Is that bad?'

'No, Alex, it isn't bad,' Darth Daver jumped in. 'You should wear whatever you like. You look very nice.'

'Thanks, Double-D. You look very tall and long-haired, like a young Professor Snape.'

'Thanks, dude.'

'Ooh, and if I'm Harry Potter and you're Professor Snape, that must mean Jess is…'

'I'm nothing like Hermione Granger, thanks very much!' Jess glared at me.

'Actually, I was going to say Dobby the Elf. Awkward.'

For the first time ever, Jess's cheeks went red. 'Stop laughing, Dave.'

'Come on, Jess, you do have pointy pixie ears, and the big eyes.' Dave was laughing so hard, he was struggling to get the words out.

'And she's super-small, don't forget. You are super-small, Jess,' I said.

'Shut up, Alex.'

'Jeez, I was only talking about the way you look, not your personality or anything.'

Jess stomped off ahead, leaving Darth Daver and me to walk into the playground together.

He was still smiling. 'I'm glad we're friends, Alex.'

At that moment I realised two very important things: one – my ear didn't fart, and two – I was glad too. Really glad.

Jess had calmed down by the time I saw her walking to the hall for the morning PALS session, so I decided to run her through my latest plan.

'We could make badges that say "I love PALS" and hand them out. Anyone who takes one must be One Of Them. I've seen a badge-making machine on eBay for just £159.99, with free postage.'

Jess sighed.

'What? Didn't you hear me say "free postage"?'

'Let me just check my pockets. Surely I have £159.99 weighing them down that I've been wanting to waste on a STUPID PLAN.'

'Hey! What's so stupid about it?'

'Apart from the obvious £159.99-sized flaw, there's the fact that it isn't accurate enough. How would we know for sure that the kids wearing the badges were all blueberries? Here's a life lesson for you: people will take *anything* if it's free.'

'Maybe we could charge 50p? Nobody would spend 50p on a PALS badge except someone who really loved PALS. We might even make a profit! We can go halves: I'll get a new Wii U game and you can give your share to the lame hedgehog society.'

'What a rubbish idea! We'll get caught and end up in the PALS room getting changed like the rest of them. Besides, it'd take days to make the badges and sell them and we're running out of time.'

I was about to give Jess a talking to about how wrong it is for her to try to crush my entrepreneurial spirit, but we'd reached the hall and it was spookily silent. That's when we saw them.

'Woah.'

Jess' eyes were wide as she looked around the hall at the rows and rows of kids waiting for the PALS session to begin. 'So that's what a blueberry wears on Mufti Day: school uniform.'

I guess wearing your own clothes to school is not in the PALS handbook. It would be too much freedom. The blueberries don't want to stand out and be different; they want to be the same, all the time, in every way. Kids choosing to wear uniform on Mufti Day – it was messed up.

As the classes filed in the sick feeling that had started in my gut when we reached the hall grew stronger and stronger. We'd wanted to know what we were up against. We'd wanted to know how many kids had been turned into blueberries. Now we had the answer.

There were hundreds of them.

Miss Smilie stood at the front of the hall, her shadow, which was ten times her size, looming over us from the giant screen.

'I have a wonderful announcement,' she said. 'On the last day before half term, we will be holding a special assembly to celebrate the achievements of PALS. All of your parents will be invited to attend so they can see for themselves the improvements that have been made in attendance levels, test results and behaviour.'

She grinned so hard that I swear I could see her shadow grinning too.

The PALS pals beamed at each other. The normal kids looked down and said nothing. A few weeks ago there would have been groans and rolling eyes, but things had changed and everyone knew it.

Jess's eyes met mine and I knew exactly what

she was thinking: first the PALpod delivery and now the assembly. It couldn't be a coincidence.

In spite of the odd tricky moment, I'd always assumed that Jess and I would find a way to stop Miss Smilie. After all, the good guys always find a way to beat the baddies – everyone knows that. But for the first time, I felt like it was slipping away from us. We still didn't know exactly how Smilie was blueberrying the kids, or how we could stop her. And we only had just over a week until the assembly. We were running out of time.

We spent break and lunchtime going over everything again and again. What had we missed? What else could we do? There must be a way.

When I sat down for afternoon PALS, everything seemed normal – blinds down, lights dimmed, the big screen set up at the front with the usual images projected on it. But when the music came on, it wasn't the normal music. It came on so loudly that it made me really jump, and everyone else too from what I could see. And it wasn't the gentle PALS tunes, it was electric-guitar rock music with shouty singing over the top. It had swears and everything. How had this happened?

A few kids started quietly sniggering as Miss Smilie stormed to the front of the hall. I put my hand over my mouth to cover up my massive smile. But then I noticed the PALS pals.

Every kid wearing school uniform was freaking out.

They had all turned pale and wide-eyed. They all looked upset. Some of them put their hands over their ears and manically shook their heads while others banged their heads into their hands, hard. They rubbed and scratched at their skin and some wrapped their arms around their bellies and groaned. It was super weird.

But then the music stopped.

'EVERYBODY BACK TO YOUR CLASS-ROOMS! NOW!' Miss Smilie screamed down the hall.

I stood up and started walking towards the door, taking one last look over my shoulder at Smilie.

She was standing at the front of the hall by her laptop, her back to the room, her hands by her side with her fists clenched. From the back she looked completely still, but I was pretty sure that was just to hide the fact that she was about to Hulk out.

'Alex Sparrow and Jessica Lawler, you will remain behind,' she said, without turning round.

Gulp. Why do people always assume that I'm responsible when someone's done something naughty? I know I quite often am responsible, but this time it was totally not me.

'Will the last person to leave the room, please shut the door?' she called out.

Everyone shuffled out of the room in silence, some of them shooting us 'I-bet-you're-pooing-your-pants' looks. In a minute, the hall was empty, and the bang of the closing door echoed around the room.

'I suppose you're pleased with yourselves,' she said, as she started x-ing out of the windows she had open on her computer.

'Was it you?' Jess mouthed behind her back.

I shook my head.

Smilie stayed silent, her face hidden, her fingers clicking on her mousepad.

Jess raised both eyebrows and pouted at me.

I made an annoyed gesture with my hands and gave her the stink-eye.

'Really?' she mouthed.

'Honest!' I mouthed back, pointing at her nose

and doing a long, exaggerated sniff. No stink equals no lie. Even she couldn't argue with that.

Still Smilie didn't turn round or speak. It was chilling.

'Who?' Jess mouthed.

I shrugged.

'Ooh,' Jess mouthed, pulling a hairband off her wrist and using it to tie her hair up in a messy knot on her head.

'What you doing?' I mouthed back, pointing my fingers at my head and twiddling them round in the crazy circles.

Jess made mouths out of her hands, wobbling her head around so that bits of her hair started falling down while mouthing 'Blah, blah, blah.'

'Oh!' I nodded, making finger glasses and holding them up to my eyes. 'You think it was The Prof?' I mouthed.

Jess shrugged a maybe.

I shook my head. 'Don't think so,' I mouthed. 'Too risky.'

Miss Smilie still wasn't saying anything. Clearly about to Hulk out.

Jess pointed at Smilie's back and lifted her hands, palms up, with a questioning look on her face.

'Roaaaaar,' I mouthed, slow-motion stomping, messing up my hair and pulling at my clothes, pretending to rip them off. A button popped off my shirt and dropped onto the floor. 'Oh, bums,' I said out loud. 'Mum's going to kill me later.'

'Not if I kill you first,' Miss Smilie said, with a sinister little psychopath laugh. She finally turned around.

Her face wasn't green. I was a bit disappointed.

'Do you think I'm annoyed by this stunt, Alex?' she said, taking a couple of steps towards us.

'Er, yes?'

'I'm not.'

'Really, Miss? You seem a bit wound up.'

'Practical jokes played by silly little boys don't bother me.' She moved closer.

'How do you know it was a boy that did it?' I said. 'Bit sexist, Miss.'

'This has your name written all over it.'

'I don't know how because it wasn't me.'

'It wasn't him!' Jess shouted.

'Well, you would say that, wouldn't you, Jessica?' Smilie snarled, still prowling towards us. 'You two have been joined at the hip lately. I can't decide if it's nauseatingly sweet or just very suspicious.'

'She's not my girlfriend or anything, Miss,' I piped in quickly.

Jess snorted.

'Partners in crime, then?' Miss Smilie said, looking from me, to Jess and back again.

We both backed away.

'You can't just assume it was us,' Jess said. 'You have no proof. And you can't keep us in here. Let us go or I'll report you.'

'It will be my word against yours. You have no proof either, Jessica,' Smilie smiled.

'Other than the recording of this conversation that I've been making on my phone, you mean?' Jess wiggled her iPhone at Miss Smilie.

And that's when stuff really went cray-cray.

Smilie stormed across the room like a rampaging elephant, dressed in purple sportswear.

Me and Jess backed quickly away until we reached the corner of the room. There was nowhere left to go. We stood side by side as she thundered towards us.

What we needed was some kind of force field, but unfortunately The Professor had only given me a farting ear and not the kind of proper superpower that would actually have been helpful in a dangerous situation.

Smilie's arm lashed out at Jess, making her flinch. (Not me, obviously, I am a highly trained agent and was well prepared for her attack, like a coiled snake with one eye open.) She swatted the phone out of Jess's hand and it hit the floor with a crunch.

'Oops,' Smilie smiled.

Jess stomped her boot down hard on Smilie's perfectly clean pink trainer, leaving a large black smear all over it. 'Oops,' she smiled back. She ran over to where her phone lay on the floor.

Smilie was angrier than I'd ever seen her, and if there's one thing I've learnt about using my power it's that it works best when people are wound up.

I looked at Miss Smilie. 'What's your problem with the music, anyway?'

'I have no problem with any music, but it is against school rules to play unauthorised music on the premises.'

'Since when?'

'Since the school started working towards a better future.'

'But why?'

'Because it upsets the atmosphere of tranquility which is vital for creating optimum learning conditions.'

'Are you sure it isn't because it makes some of the kids unwell?'

She gave me the gobbler look again. 'I don't know what you're talking about.'

Lie.

'I'm talking about how when the rock music played instead of the PALS music, it made some of the kids, *certain* kids, act a bit weird. You know, shaking, crying, rubbing their stomachs… Was the music making them ill?'

'Of course not, ridiculous child.'

Lie.

Jess sniffed and looked from me to Smilie.

'There has been a virus circulating the school,' Smilie said. 'Any children looking unwell are no doubt suffering the symptoms of it.'

Lie.

'It's a nasty bug. You must know – you and Jessica were suffering from it just the other day.'

'So if I was to play all those kids a load of rock music, for a longer time, say for five or ten minutes, it wouldn't make them ill?'

'No. Of course not.'

Lie.

'Maybe tomorrow whoever changed the music – a.k.a. NOT ME – should change the video clip to something more exciting, let's say *Star Wars*, for example. Or might that get those kids feeling all "virusy" again? Hmm?'

'No. No. NO! Nobody will be tampering with the PALS resources again, because you and Miss Lawler are going to be dealt with once and for all, in the PALS suite. Now!'

How the heck were we going to get out of this? Jess looked at the door and started tapping at her phone. Who the heck was she going to call? I didn't think the police would believe us and I was pretty sure she didn't have The Avengers on speed dial.

'This is outrageously unfair!' I said, stalling, thinking, hoping for a way out. 'How can you punish us without proof?'

I don't need proof if I get a confession,' she said, coming so close to me that the zip of her tracksuit was brushing against my jumper. She leaned over me, putting a hand against the wall on either side of my head. I couldn't move. 'Things will be much better for you, Alex Sparrow, if you just tell the truth.'

'He is telling the truth,' Jess shouted. 'Trust me, we'd know all about it if he wasn't.'

Miss Smilie moved her face in closer, so that we were nose to nose, her breath blowing right onto my skin. Funny how something warm can give you the shivers. And by funny, I mean not funny at all and actually very creepy. I could basically hear her seething.

'Confess,' she hissed at me.

'Let me think about it for a moment...' I said. 'Er, no.'

'Then maybe I'll have to find another way to make you co-operate.'

A bit of her spit went in my eye.

'Gross,' Jess said.

'By spitting at me, Miss?' I said. 'I'm pretty sure that is unauthorised teacher behaviour. I'm going to have to run it by the Head, my mum and dad and maybe the local authorities, I'm afraid.'

I met Jess's gaze and nodded towards the door, telling her to run for it and save herself, but she shook her head.

'Run it by whoever you like, Alex. People will

laugh at you. They'll put it down to the delusions of a silly, attention-seeking child. A letter will be going out to the whole school this afternoon, warning parents about the virus. Nobody will believe a word you say.'

'Whatevs, Miss. By the way, you've got a bit of lipstick on your teeth. You might want to pop to the toilets and sort yourself out.'

'Impudent boy!' she screamed, slamming her hands against the wall by my ears.

'Calm down, Miss, doesn't PALS stand for "Peace And Love, Son"?'

'PALS stands for Positive Aspirational Life Skills, as you know. Skills that you are sorely missing.'

I was just about to tell her I'd be making a detailed statement about her outrageous actions and sending them to Ofsted, and one of those 'no-win-no-fees' lawyers from the TV, but I hesitated. Miss Smilie had just lied. She said 'PALS stands for Positive Aspirational Life Skills', and my ear buzzed. I forgot my confusion when the door to the hall opened, and Darth Daver walked in.

'It was me, Miss Smilie, I changed the music. I've already told the Head and he sent me here to report to you. Alex and Jess had nothing to do with it. He said to send them back to class and give me whatever punishment seems appropriate.'

'Dave, no! What are you doing?' Jess looked terrified.

Miss Smilie let go of my hand and turned to Darth Daver. She seemed torn between reluctance to let me and Jess go and excitement at getting her hands on Darth Daver.

'Alex and Jessica, get back to your classrooms. I'll deal with your friend.'

We hesitated. We couldn't leave him. How could we leave him?

'Alex and Jessica, get out of my sight or I'll take all three of you to the PALS suite, regardless of what the Head says.'

'You guys should go.' Darth Daver turned to Jess and me. 'It isn't fair for you to get punished for something you didn't do.' With his back to Miss Smilie, Darth Daver held his hand out to Jess. As she took it, he gave us the bravest, saddest smile I've ever seen and silently mouthed two words: 'Trust me.'

Miss Smilie was practically dribbling at the thought of getting Darth Daver back to her lair. I guess he was probably a prime target for her, with his long hair, one fingernail painted black and in his dark mufti clothes; he was different from everybody else. I used to think he was weird and scummy, but he was the sweetest guy in the world, one of my best friends and the last person I wanted to see being turned into another boring blueberry.

'OUT, NOW!' Miss Smilie screamed.

Darth Daver let go of Jess's hand and nodded. She turned and pulled me towards the hall doors and out into the corridor, tears pouring down her cheeks. I had never seen Jess cry before. She didn't really seem the crying type. It was awful.

'What is up with you and him? Always doing The Right Thing – it's so flipping frustrating! We have to go back. We have to stop it!' I said.

'No. He asked me to trust him. And he gave me this.' Jess opened her hand to show me a folded-up piece of paper. It was a note from Darth Daver.

We locked ourselves in a boy's toilet cubicle, opened the piece of paper and while Jess sobbed, I read.

Jess and Alex,

I don't have much time to write this, so I hope it makes sense.

It doesn't take a genius to realise that there's some bad stuff going on in this school. Things have been weird for a while now, but when I saw all the PALS kids wearing uniform this morning, I knew it had gone too far. I had to do something to show we're not all mindless clones yet, so I hacked into the computer system and switched Smilie's PALS music.

I'm handing myself in because I'm responsible for what happened and should be the one who gets punished. I'm also handing myself in because I can't let you guys end up like the others. Whatever's going on around here, something tells me that you two know more about it than anyone else, and that you have to be the ones to fix everything.

I get the feeling I'm not going to be the same after my detention with Miss Smilie, so I'll leave you with the only thing I have that might help – her computer password: xxmontyxx

Please don't worry about me, just take that control freak down.

You're my best friends, I know you'll find a way.

Dave x

17

We Hit The Bottom

Darth Daver was excluded for the rest of the day, so Jess and I didn't see him until the following morning. As we waited at the gate, Jess couldn't keep still. She paced back and forth and bit her lip. Her eyes were red and puffy. He hadn't replied to her texts so we knew it was going to be bad. We knew, but somehow we weren't prepared at all.

Darth Daver was the tallest kid in school, so we saw him coming from a long way off. Even from a distance, he looked like a different boy.

'They cut his hair!' Jess said, her eyes filling with tears.

'It's so … short,' I was shocked. 'I don't think I've ever seen his whole face before.'

Darth Daver was really shy, so he had always hidden behind his long hair. He was also self-conscious about his height, so he usually hunched over a bit, almost as if he was trying to make himself smaller.

'He's walking weird. Why is he walking like that?' Jess was getting more upset by the second.

'He's just standing up straight, Jess.' I tried to reassure her.

'He's not even trying to cover his hands.' She was sobbing now. 'I always tell him not to cover them because he shouldn't be ashamed of his skin condition, but he never listens.'

'Then at least he's not embarrassed by it anymore. I guess that's kind of a good thing?' I was trying to help but it wasn't working.

'Where's his schoolbag that we decorated together with lyrics from our favourite songs? Where are his shoes that he scuffed when he tried to kick that football last week and fell over instead? It's like everything that made him Dave is gone. There's nothing good about any of this. Nothing!'

Darth Daver walked towards us, smiling that awful PALS smile, and when he reached me and Jess, he just carried on walking past without so much as looking at us.

It was heartbreaking.

I wanted to make Jess feel better but I didn't know what to say, so I put my arm around her and we walked to the school door in silence. Her face was streaked with glistening lines from her tears, and every now and then she choked as she tried to hold back another sob. She looked smaller and sort of broken.

By the time I got to my classroom, I was determined to take action. If I could get some new information or evidence to help us stop Miss Smilie and fix Dave, maybe I could give Jess back some hope.

'Miss Fortress,' I said, as soon as the register had been taken, 'do you remember I was asking you about a special project?'

Miss Fortress looked confused but she tried to play along. 'The special project about…'

'…that famous painting of that lady with dark

hair – the Moaning Lisa is it? You know – the woman with the *weird smile.*' Excellent code talk, Agent Alex.

'Oh, yes, Alex, I do recall that. Don't you think we're better off discussing this after class?'

'Normally, yes, but this is super-important research and I need to do it on a school computer.'

'You could borrow my laptop?'

'If I borrow your laptop, it might look like *you've done the work.*' I tried to give her a wink (Important Agent Note: need to practise my winks.) If I was going to access Smilie's files, it needed to be from a computer that couldn't be traced back to any of us. 'It would be better if we could do it in, say, the IT hub.'

'It's funny you should mention that, Alex, because I was planning to have our first lesson this morning in the IT hub.'

She wasn't very subtle, but nobody seemed to notice.

'Come on, class, we're going to do some group work in the IT hub. It will involve a lot of loud talking.'

Once everyone was busy in the hub, grouped

around computers, Miss Fortress set me up in the corner.

'What can I help you with?' she asked.

'I need to log in as Miss Smilie and copy her PALS files. I don't know how to hack, although Darth Daver did apparently, which would have been good to know a couple of weeks ago. Anyway, I have her password.'

'Do you have something to save the files on? A USB stick?'

'No, Miss, like I said, I'm not the hacker of our team.'

'This is the only one I have spare. You can borrow it but I'd like it back when you're finished.'

She pulled a USB out of her pocket. It had a picture of Thor on it with no top on.

'You're like the most inappropriate teacher in the world, Miss, do you know that?'

'Let's be quick about this. We can't afford to get caught. Are you looking for anything specific?'

'Maybe something to do with a guy called Montgomery McMonaghan,' I said.

Miss Fortress gasped and dropped the USB.

'What is it?' I said.

'Montgomery McMonaghan was my lab partner. The one I'm hiding from.'

'Then we definitely need to find out more.'

Miss Fortress showed me how to log on as a member of staff, so I held my breath and entered Smilie's password.

'Boom, we're in!' I said, as Miss Smilie's files started loading. 'I am swag level nine thousand.'

'Because you entered a password correctly?' Miss Fortress said, in a tone which suggested she wasn't very impressed with my skillz.

'Because I did it with style, Miss. Jeez, you're as bad as Jess.'

'Just focus on the task, Alex. Find the files you need and copy them before we get caught.'

'Yep – deffo another fun-sucker,' I said, clicking on the folder labelled 'PALS'.

It was empty.

Thinking she might have hidden the files under a code name, I tried another. Also empty. I went through the folders one by one. They were all empty.

'Son of a biscuit!' I banged the mouse down on the desk.

'She must have deleted them,' Miss Fortress said.

'After the thing in the hall when the music was switched, she was clicking around for ages on her laptop.'

'She probably saved them onto her hard drive, or a memory stick, as a security measure.'

'So if we want to get those files…'

'You'll need access to her laptop.'

'Then that's what I'll do,' I said.

'But you'll have to get into her office! How on earth are you going to do that?'

'I'll have to come up with something,' I said. 'I am super-good at plans, just FYI.'

'I haven't seen much evidence of that so far. She's been one step ahead of you at every turn.'

'We got you a PALpod, didn't we?'

'I suppose,' she frowned. 'I've been analysing the device and it seems it's been created to apply the Neuro-Electric Impulse Transmutation Procedure to the user.'

'The what?'

'The spark in the ear thing,' Miss Fortress sighed.

'Oh,' I said. 'That's super-bad.'

'That's both an oxymoron and an understate-ment.'

'No need for the insults, Miss,' I said. Between her and Jess it was surprising that I had any self-esteem left at all. 'When we get the files, which we will when I come up with a genius plan, what should we look out for? What sorts of things could be feeding the sparked kids the blueberry information?'

'Look out for subliminal messages.'

'What is that? Some kind of underwater thing?'

'Not submarinal, subliminal. It means hidden messages. When I was young there was a big thing about backmasked music: when we played some of our records backwards, we could hear voices telling us to worship the devil.'

'It must have been crazy bad in the olden days.'

'Of course, Miss Smilie would need certain equipment to get the messages in backwards.'

'Actually, I'm pretty sure there's an app for that, Miss.'

Miss Fortress looked disgusted and started muttering something about apps replacing scientists and the end of the world.

'Miss,' I said, 'how did you get into the PALS suite the other day, when Smilie was trying to shut me in the tasting-slash-testing room?'

'Mr Crumpet let me in. He has spare keys for every room in the school.'

'Hm…' I said.

'Do you have a plan?' Miss Fortress asked.

'Yes,' I said. 'I'm having crumpets when I get home from school.'

Miss Fortress stomped off.

When I met Jess at break, she looked defeated.

'How are you doing?' I asked, even though it was pretty clear that she was doing rubbish. What else could I say?

'I've had to sit next to Dave all day. He lines all his pencils up in a perfect row on his desk, he raises his hand to answer questions and he doesn't talk to me. It's as if he never even knew me.'

'I'm sorry, Jess.'

'It's so hard. It's like the real Dave never existed.'

I put my arm around her. 'The good news is that Miss Fortress is making progress with the PALpod. And there's something else. Back in the hall, when Miss Smilie tried to assassinate me…'

'You mean when she stood quite close to you,' Jess said.

'…when she had me against the wall in a death grip…' I said.

'I wouldn't describe it as a death grip.'

'That's because you like to make everything seem as boring as possible, Jessticles,' I said. 'Anyway, you know what she said about the meaning of PALS? She was lying.'

'But if it doesn't mean what we all think it means, then what *does* it mean?'

'That, my trusty sidekick, is what we need to find out. We really need Smilie's computer.'

'That'll be easy, then,' Jess said.

'Fear not, Jessticles. I have an amazing plan.'

18

The Plan

'It was the most complicated plan yet. It required courage, speed and precise timing. And also a stinking ear and collaboration with a pigeon. In other words, Agent Alex and The Creature Feature were the perfect agents for the job.'

'Shut up, Alex!' Jess said. 'Narrating what we're doing when we're supposed to be hiding is beyond stupid. Even for you.'

'Just trying to add some swag, Jessticles.'

'And don't call me The Creature Feature.'

We were leaning against the wall around the corner from the caretaker's office, waiting for Miss Fortress, who was providing a diversion. Although, to be honest, it was tough even getting her to do that, what with all the fuss about her secret identity.

She'd dropped a test tube of something that looked like snot on the floor in her classroom while I stood over it and whipped up an enormous stink. Jess and I then made our way to Mr Crumpet's office, leaving a stink trail as we went. We were just waiting for Miss Fortress to carry out the next step in the plan.

'There's no way Mr Crumpet is in the League of Villains with Smilie, is there?'

'First,' Jess huffed, 'stop giving everything stupid names. Second, there is absolutely no way Mr Crumpet is a villain. He's worked here for a million years and he's about eighty. And third, shut up, Agent Annoying, Miss Fortress is coming.'

'If she's coming, then you should be keeping quiet,' I whispered. 'And Agent Annoying is a terrible name.'

We watched Miss Fortress take a deep breath

and then bang on Mr Crumpet's door in an extra-urgent way. He opened it surprisingly quickly, considering he was about a hundred and twenty.

'Please come immediately, Mr Crumpet,' Miss Fortress said. 'There's been a chemical spillage in my classroom. I require assistance. At once.'

Mr Crumpet nodded and turned back into his office.

'No, no, Mr Crumpet, there's no time. Can't you smell the toxic fumes?'

He sniffed the air and made a face.

'There is an extreme risk of … injury and disfigurement!' Miss Fortress shrieked, grabbing his arm and pulling him down the corridor.

'Let's go,' Jess said, and we ran to Mr Crumpet's open cupboard-slash-office. On his desk was a massive bunch of keys with little labels attached.

'Which one is it?' I asked.

'How should I know, dufus? We'll have to look through one by one.'

Jess started at one end, while I worked from the other. There were literally about a hundred keys to go through, and I started to sweat, thinking that any second Mr Crumpet would come back.

'Got it!' I said. I tried to pull it off the keyring,

but it was really stiff. We'd come all this way, only to be defeated by a metal ring. I felt furious that I hadn't been provided with a laser watch for this kind of situation. I bet James Bond didn't have to put up with this kind of low-budget treatment.

'Give it here, Alex,' Jess snatched it away from me. 'Let me try.'

'No offence, Jessticles,' I said, 'but you're just a girl. Without super-strength or Magneto's metal-moving abilities, I don't think you're going to manage it.'

'Got it!' she said, dangling the stupid key in front of me. 'Who needs superpowers when you have the strength of a normal girl?'

'I must have loosened it for you,' I said.

Jess rolled her eyes. 'So I guess we'd better split up.'

We looked at each other for a moment. I have to admit, I was a little nervous about carrying out the next phase of the plan without Jess. I didn't want her to know that, though.

'Woah! You're not going to try to kiss me are you?' I said. 'Because that's going to be totally awkward. I can't blame you for wanting to. I am, after all, irresistible, but I just don't look at you that way.'

'You're infuriating,' she said and turned to leave.

'Jess,' I called after her.

'What?'

'May the force be with you.'

'Good luck, Alex,' she said and ran off towards the playground where we had hidden Miss Smilie's tracking device.

I took the key and made my way to the corridor that led to the PALS suite, where I hid and waited. The next part of the mission was in Jess's hands.

The seconds passed by slowly. My heart was thumping in my chest and my hands were sweating. I imagined myself running with Jess, down the corridors, past the hall, the library, the classrooms and out into the playground. Then, over to the Friendship Bench to collect the tracker and down the side of the school to where Dexter was waiting to take it, fly up past the fire escape and drop it on the roof. Add a couple of minutes to allow for the delay on the bird-poo-disabled device, and Miss Smilie should come out of the PALS suite any time…

I heard the door open and someone walking quickly up the corridor. I held my breath and flattened myself against the wall as Miss Smilie went past. It was time to move.

I slunk into the PALS suite and made my way to Smilie's office, praying that Jess had chosen the correct key. I put it in the keyhole and tried to turn it, but it got stuck and my sweaty hand slipped off the metal. We'd only got the wrong flipping one! Then I realised I had put it in upside down. I tried again and this time, the lock clicked and the door opened. Well done, Agent Alex.

Miss Smilie's laptop was on her desk. I was a bit afraid to touch it in case it was booby trapped, but I imagined Jess telling me not to be so stupid. I turned it on, entered the password, and I was in.

It didn't take long to find the files – Miss Smilie obviously thought her office was uninfiltrateable. Ha! Not when Agent Alex is around. I plugged in the Thor stick, and started copying the files. As I waited for them to upload, I looked around Smilie's office to distract myself from the panic that might have been rising up inside me, if I wasn't a professional agent who never panics in any situation. It was like PALS central in there: all posters of sunsets and cornfields with affirmations written over the top. There was one photo on her desk of a man with blacky-grey curly hair and really wide-open, glinty eyes which seemed to be looking right at me. It proper gave me the creeps, so I tried not to look at it. On a shelf above her desk was a pile of memory sticks with the PALS logo on. I know it was a risk but I put one in my pocket. It might come in handy later. At last the final file uploaded. I unplugged and left the room, locking the door behind me.

When I reached the Friendship Bench, Jess was waiting.

'I hope you didn't mess your part up,' she said.

'Good to see you, too, sweetness.'

'No problems?' she said.

'For once, my only problem is you.'

'Ditto.'

'Did she find the tracker?'

Jess laughed, for the first time since Darth Daver became Blueberry Dave. 'Yeah, I was watching from behind the big cherry tree. She found it, threw a bit of a fit, said some very unPALSy words and jumped on it about twenty times. I think her hair even moved a bit.'

'No. Way.'

'I wish you could have seen it,' she smiled at me.

'So it's gone?'

'I'd say so.'

'Thank fudge,' I said. 'I hated carrying that thing around.'

'Me too,' she said. 'Meet you after school?'

'Affirmative.'

After school, Mum and Lauren went out to tidy the garden, so me and Jess put my laptop on the breakfast bar, where Bob could see it too, and I plugged in half-naked Thor. We loaded the first PALS music track and literally held our breath as we set it up to play backwards. So much depended on us hearing something incriminating.

A couple of seconds in, a voice started saying things like, 'Be happy and proud to be part of a crowd,' 'Only fools don't follow the rules,' 'You'll always be in style if you don't forget to smile,' and a load of other stupid rhymes like the rubbish the blueberries had been spouting. There were lots to do with being positive, which weren't so bad, but also a lot about never challenging authority or questioning anything. Stuff like, 'You'll only be cool if you don't break a rule' and how it's 'always best to be the same as the rest'.

Next we clicked on one of the image clips. We played it at slower than normal speed so we could try to spot any hidden images. At first we saw nothing, and were going to move on to the next one, but Bob started waggling his fins at us.

'He saw something. He said to try again.'

We slowed it down even more and watched. In between the usual PALS images of trees blowing in the breeze and fish darting in and out of coral there were other images: a bunch of teenagers jumping up and down at a concert; kids wearing hoodies and riding skateboards, a girl with blue hair and a piercing in her nose. After each of the hidden images came up, they were followed by a picture of a man: a man with a disapproving and very familiar face, giving the image a big thumbs down. It was Simon Cowell.

Jess was really, really angry.

'How can she do this? She takes the most amazing people, electric shocks away everything that makes them special and turns them into mass-produced, plastic nothingness. She's like a sports version of Professor Umbridge. I hate her!'

She started to cry again.

'We'll beat her, Jess. This is good evidence. We'll show everyone at the assembly. People will have to listen.'

'Will they, though? What if the parents just see the better test results and their kids always doing what they're told and decide they like it that way?'

'I don't think they'd like seeing the PALS freaking out if they listen to non-PALS music.' That's when I had my idea – the way we were going to expose Smilie. The final showdown. 'Here's what we're going to do. We're going to get all this evidence together and then we're going to make a clip of our own. Something with really inappropriate music.'

'An anti-PALS clip?'

'Exactly. Then we're going to crash the assembly and show everyone there what Smilie's been up to.'

Jess sniffed. 'That could work, I suppose. But what if it isn't doesn't?'

Time to rally the troops. 'Here's how this is going to end: Miss Smilie will get thrown in jail; you'll get Darth Daver back, and I'll finally get the respect and recognition I deserve for being a world-class, superstar bad-A. That's what's happening, that's how it's going down, failure is not an option.'

'But…'

'No buts.'

'What if…'

'No what ifs.'

'You're being annoying.'

'Maybe so, but the question remains: are you with me, sister?'

'But…'

'I said no buts. I don't know about you, Jessticles, but I can keep this up all day.'

'Fine.'

'Say the words.'

'I'm with you.'

'…brother.'

'But you're not…'

'Say it.'

'I'm with you. Brother.'

'That's the spirit! Fist bump?'

Jess huffed and whacked me in the arm.

Jess came over every day that week, so we could work on our presentation. My mum seemed to think we were in love or something disgusting like that. She kept making gooey faces and talking in a weird voice – so annoying. But luckily it meant she gave us some privacy, as long as we stayed in the kitchen with the door open. Jess's mum was "cool with it", apparently. She and Jess were all about the trust.

With the PALS assembly only days away, we found ourselves counting down with a mix of dread and excitement. It was like waiting for Christmas Day, if Christmas Day involved having to make your way through a jungle of man-eating gorillas to get to your presents.

Each day we felt the pressure weighing on us a little more. We stayed up late into the evenings – or as late as we could get away with before my mum made Jess go home – going through Smilie's computer files. We were looking for anything else that might help us, but specifically something to do with the meaning of PALS. Unfortunately, almost every file had the word PALS in it a billion times, so it wasn't until the night before the assembly that we found it.

It was a document Miss Smilie had created: a PALS sign-up sheet. There was a bit at the beginning about how unbelievably brilliant PALS is, followed by this:

'I hereby give parental consent for my son or daughter(s) to be enrolled onto the PALS scheme, with immediate effect. I will co-operate with the school in any way deemed necessary to help my child progress through the programme and accept the complimentary PALpod to enable my child to continue their work at home. I understand that in signing this form, I have agreed to the terms and conditions.*'

'It looks harmless, written like that,' I said.

'Would you have preferred her to have used a more sinister font? Perhaps giant letters with blood dripping down them?'

'That would have been super-helpful, actually. I expect you use the font of misery whenever you're typing stuff up.'

'Only when I'm typing stuff up about you.'

'Shush, Jessticles, I'm trying to concentrate,' I said, reading it through again. 'So basically, Miss Smilie is going to get the parents of every kid in school to sign their children up for PALS.'

'And to take home a PALpod which will spark them all...' Jess's eyes widened.

'So they're just a power-on away from matching smiles and sensible haircuts.'

We looked at each other. This was bad.

'What's after that?' Jess asked.

'Loads of empty pages for the parents' signatures and then a page of terms and conditions in teeny tiny writing.'

'Remember what Miss Fortress said about always reading them?'

'I remember what happened last time we didn't read them,' I said. 'I'll get us a snack and then we'll get started.'

I snuck down to the fridge and pinched a can of my dad's Red Bull. Yeah, yeah, I know I shouldn't have and, to be honest, it tasted disgusting so we only had a couple of sips, but that was all we needed. We went back to work.

Jess would tell you we found it at exactly the same time, but I'm pretty sure I got there a second before her.

'I can't believe it!' I said.

'I know!' Jess gasped.

'That's quite a lie!'

'It's an enormous lie!'

'It's the Death Star, nay, the Starkiller of lies!'

'Did you just say "nay"?' Jess looked at me.

'Focus, Jessticles,' I said.

We stared at the screen. It had been in front of us all along, but nobody had noticed.

'Well, this should get people's attention,' Jess said.

I imagined the parents going angry-mob mental on Smilie's butt.

'Even better,' I smiled. 'This should get people MAD.'

19

Jess Kicks Balls, Bob Slaps Face, And I Embarrass My Mum

It was the final day before half term. Jess and I went to morning registration as usual but snuck away from our classes as they filed down the corridors to the hall for assembly. It was a warm day, so windows and doors were open all over the school and I was starting to sweat.

Jess was carrying Bob in his jar. We'd brought him along because he might come in handy and, anyway, we couldn't leave him out of the final battle: he was part of the unit.

A grey blur suddenly whizzed past my face and made me jump. It was Dexter. He spoke to Jess for less than a minute and then flew off. I knew something was wrong because he didn't poo on me.

'What's happened?'

'He came to warn us. Miss Fortress has been told she has to attend the assembly. She can't risk blowing her cover, so she won't be able to help us, no matter how bad it gets. Miss Smilie has people out looking for us, so Dexter said we have to find somewhere to lay low until we can get to the main event.'

'Oh bums! Where's he gone now?'

'He's gone to, erm, round up the boys.'

'Right.'

We hid in the last place we thought Miss Smilie would look for us: the PALS suite. It was quiet and still, apart from the whirring of the pump in the fish tank. I unpacked my rucksack – ham sandwiches, leftover Red Bull, a puzzle book for Bob and some of those foam earplugs. I thought they'd protect me from sparking. Jess thought I was stupid.

We sat down and took the lid off Bob's jar so he'd have more air and light. We just had to stay hidden until the assembly was underway. It would only be ten minutes but it felt like hours, jumping at every little sound and hoping we wouldn't get caught.

'Is this really the best we can do for a hiding place?' I said. 'Perhaps we should climb into a ventilation shaft or something?'

'Great idea! I'll get the blueprints out and maybe we can crawl all the way to the hall through a maze of tunnels!'

I sensed that Jess was being sarcastic. 'You go first then. You'll be happy in there with nothing but darkness and rats – they're two of your favourite things.'

'Well, at least I'll be able to move around in the shafts. You'll just get stuck because of your massive head.'

'Big head, big brain.' I grinned at her. And the door to the PALS room opened.

'Arguing again, I see.' Miss Smilie walked in, with Jason. Wait – what? I couldn't understand why he was there.

'Jason, you should go,' I said. 'You don't want to be in here with her.'

'I'm not going anywhere, Scuzzo. I saw you freaks coming in here, and now I get to watch you suffer.'

'You told Miss Smilie we were here?'

'Yeah, I told her.' He looked really pleased with himself. 'I've been telling her a lot of things lately.'

My first thought was that he'd been PALSified, but there was no moronic smile, no rhyming about the joy of rules and he had a big stain down his sweatshirt where he'd obviously spilt his breakfast. Still, I had to check. 'Jason, did Miss Smilie do anything weird to your ear?'

'Oh, Jason hasn't been modified,' said Miss Smilie. 'I decided he'd be more helpful to me as he is. It seems that you've been rather getting on his nerves and he was delighted to keep an eye on you for me.' She turned to Jason, 'Grab the bag, would you, Jason?'

Jason snatched the bag out of my hand.

'You're working with her?' I looked him right in the eye. 'But we were best friends. Doesn't that mean anything to you?'

'We were never best friends. I used to have to put up with your smug face and annoying comments, but thanks to Miss Smilie, I won't have to anymore.'

I knew Jason was a bit mean, but I'd never suspected he would do something like this. I was hurt. I couldn't think of anything to say.

We watched as Smilie tipped the contents of our bag onto the floor, getting carpet fluff all over my ham sandwiches.

'Aha!' She picked up the PALS memory stick I'd swiped from her office, and peered at the new label I'd made for it.

'PALS: PREPARE TO MEET YOUR DOOM,' she read out loud. 'And what's this supposed to be? A jelly bean with ears?'

'That's the *Home Alone* cat emoji, obvs,' I said.

'Thank you for returning this to me,' Smilie said, 'and thank you for labelling it so clearly. You really made it too easy for me. Stupid boy.'

She placed the stick carefully on the floor and stomped on it, grinding it slowly over and over with her heel.

'Dispose of this litter for me, Jason,' she said.

Jason grinned as he crouched down and started scraping up the pieces into his hand.

'Now you have no evidence,' Smilie said. 'All of your irritating snooping has been for nothing.'

Smilie was wearing a bright pink tracksuit with

her name written across the front in diamonds. Her smile was redder than ever – she looked like a demonic clown. I wouldn't have been surprised if she opened her mouth to reveal she'd swapped her normal teeth for vampire fangs.

'That's funny, Miss Smilie, you're wearing a tracksuit? I would have thought you'd want to look nice for your fancy assembly.' Jess was obviously in the mood for a fight. Honestly, there was no stopping that girl once she got carried away.

Miss Smilie just smiled. 'You, Jessica, are a perfect example of why the world needs PALS. So angry, so defiant. Just like your friend, David. We fixed him, though, didn't we?'

Jason sniggered and dusted his hands off into the bin.

'Ruined him, you mean, you psychotic witch.'

Blimey, Jess was really going for it.

'So your plan is to get all the parents to sign up for PALpods,' I said. 'So you can spark every kid in school and then feed them a load of rubbish to make them exactly how you want them to be?'

'Exactly, Alex. We live in a chaotic world, full of spoiled children who grow into troubled young adults. They have no manners, no discipline, no structure, and they think the world is theirs. It's time we got some order back, a hierarchy that keeps the power in the hands of those who deserve to wield it. Children should be quiet. Children should obey. I'm working for the greater good.'

'Oh, I thought you worked for the school, and maybe that Montgomery McMonaghan dude. What the heck is The Crater Hood? Some alien street gang?'

Jess rolled her eyes.

'Are you trying to be funny, Alex?' Miss Smilie said. 'Because we don't like your kind of funny. Never mind, we can fix that too.'

'You must be even more evil than I thought if you don't like bunnies. Everyone likes bunnies.'

'What on earth are you talking about, stupid boy? Have you gone mad?'

'Yeah, that's right, I'm pretty bad. I'm glad you've realised.'

'This is what he does, Miss,' Jason said. 'All the time.'

'Enough of this nonsense. I must get back to my assembly so I can make sure every parent is convinced that joining PALS is essential for their child's growth and wellbeing. This is just the first stage in the grand plan, the first step towards creating a world of people who are content to do as they're told. You two are insignificant specks, and we've had enough of you delaying us.'

Smilie looked down to unzip her bumbag, which was also pink and also had her name written across it in diamonds.

Jess leaned over and whispered to me, 'You put those ear plugs in, didn't you?'

'Sorry, Jess, I can't hear you. Got my ear plugs in. That'll show psycho Smilie.'

When Smilie looked up she was holding a PALpod.

'Let me show you what we can do for annoying boys with ear troubles, Alex. It will only take a second. It will hurt quite a lot actually, but once it's over, you'll be a much happier and more pleasant boy.'

She came towards me with the headphones, the sun through the window making the diamonds on her tracksuit twinkle and reflect rainbows on the walls. I backed into the corner. Jess jumped towards Smilie, but Jason grabbed her arm.

I looked at the earphones in Smilie's hand. They say that when people are close to death, their life flashes before their eyes. Well, that's kind of what happened to me. I replayed the past few weeks and realised that even though, when it was happening, I thought it was the worst time of my life, it was actually the best. I'd been challenged every day, in loads of exciting ways; I'd developed new skills and found stuff that I was actually good at; and, for the first time ever I had friends. Not people I hung around with and who hung around with me because we all wanted to be cool and popular, but real, proper, have-a-laugh-with, stand-by-you-and-stand-up-for-you, tell-you-the-truth friends. I wasn't going to let them down.

As I weighed up how wrong it would be to punch Smilie in the bumbag, a load of things happened at once. Jason started shouting and flapping around.

'The freak girl's having another one of those fit thingies! What do I do? What do I do?'

Jess, who was twitching in conversation with Bob, picked up a half-drunk can of Red Bull and poured it into Bob's jar.

And then Bob did the bravest thing I'd ever

seen. All in slow-mo and surrounded by a dazzling rainbow of light and colour, he launched himself out of his jar and flew through the air towards us. He slapped Smilie across the face with a thwack, the light glinting off his scales. Then he disappeared down her tracksuit top.

Smilie screamed, 'Get it out! Get it out!' and dropped the PALpod on the floor.

Smilie started slapping at herself where Bob was wriggling around under her clothes. She was trying to unzip her top, which was something I really didn't want to see.

Jess kicked Jason hard in the boy bits and grabbed my arm.

'Run, Alex!' She legged it to the door.

I dodged past Smilie and Jason, who was rolling on the floor, crying.

Miss Smilie pulled Bob out of her top and threw him at the wall. He hit it with a horrible crunch and slid to the floor.

'What about Bob? We have to go back for him, Jess. He 360 no-scoped Smilie and now he'll die!'

'He knew what he was doing. He wanted to help, Alex. It'll be for nothing if we get caught.'

As we flew out of the PALS suite and towards

the school hall, I looked back to see Smilie slip on a ham sandwich and fall over next to Jason.

'Get a grip, boy, and get after them!' she shouted at him.

'I can't!' he shouted. 'You destroyed the evidence anyway, Miss. Everyone will laugh if they tell them what they know without proof.'

'I don't care! I want those vile children!'

She jumped up again and started sprinting after us. The hall was far away and I wasn't sure how we were going to make it. But that was when another amazing thing happened. About a hundred pigeons flew into the building, through every open door and window. They swooped at Smilie in a whirlwind of claws and beaks. They pecked and pooed and flapped in her face – there was nothing she could do to get away from them.

So we ran on, down the corridor, past the IT hub, the cookery room, the library, all the way to the other end of the school where the main hall was full of people.

As we flew into the hall with a hurricane of pigeons behind us, the PALS were onstage performing a song. We went straight to the audio-visual desk and I pulled Miss Fortress's Thor memory stick out of the little hollow in my hat that Smilie had made when she planted the tracking device inside it. As the files uploaded, I jumped on the stage at the same moment that Smilie reached the hall.

The parents in the audience started asking what was going on. Some teachers tried to get to the stage but were blocked by the pigeons. The normal kids gasped and the PALS just carried on singing. Honestly: so weird – who would do that?

Jess turned off their backing track and I cleared my throat. I was proper nervous, thinking about how much trouble we could get into for a stunt like this. Possibly prison; possibly exile to a far-off place where we would have to fight polar bears and drink our own wee to survive. The PALS finally stopped singing and every person (and bird) in the room was looking at me. It was too late to wimp out.

'Hi, everyone. I'm sure you all know me: I'm Alex, Alex Sparrow.'

My mum tried to cover her face with her handbag.

'I'm here today because you've been lied to. Miss Smilie…' (I pointed her out in case some people didn't recognise her with pigeon poo on her face) '...has been using PALS to control your kids. Want to know how? She uses a scientific procedure which I like to call "sparking" to freeze the parts of the brain related to free will and creative thinking. Then she feeds us music and videos full of subliminal messages to brainwash us. I could tell you a story about muffins which would explain this in a bit more detail, but I don't have much time now, so ask me after if you especially want to know. My sidekick and I have prepared a short video to demonstrate. That's right, Miss Smilie, you destroyed a decoy memory stick. Classic mistake. Jessticles: show them the madness.'

As the backmasked music started playing, I could hear people gasp and start to mutter to each other. But here came the big guns. The PALS visuals flickered onto the big screen. We'd slowed them right down so that everyone could see what Bob had shown us. They saw the hidden images. They saw Simon Cowell.

As the room settled into shocked silence, I continued.

'Now, some of you may be thinking "where's

the harm? If it means little Johnny will do his homework on time and not throw a strop when I won't let him have a Happy Meal, surely that's a good thing?" Well I'm here to tell you that it is NOT a good thing.

'If you take away our freedom of thought, you'll be depriving the world of a future full of possibility. Sure, you may spare yourself the odd Kanye, but you'll also sacrifice the Vincent Van Goghs, the Martin Luther Kings, the Florence Nightingales and the Dyson vacuum cleaner men. All people who thought outside the box and did something amazing for the world.

'All I ask is that you give us the chance you had. The chance to make mistakes, to be ourselves and to exceed your expectations. To infinity and beyond.'

Time to seal the deal, ace the test, put one in the back of the net.

'Many of you parents and "so-called" guardians have been signing a form giving Miss Smilie permission to turn your kids into PALS. I'm sure you're all feeling pretty bad right now. Well, hold onto your pants because you're about to feel a lot worse.

'As Yoda probably said, after he signed up to be a Jedi and realised he'd never be allowed to party again: "The terms and conditions, always read you must." Put your hand up if you read the terms and conditions on the back of the form.'

A few people started to raise their hands.

I looked at each of them. 'It's important that you tell the truth.'

The hands went back down.

'I'm glad to hear it, because if you had read them, you'd know what you were signing your kids up for. And I'd hate to think that any of you would agree to this.'

Jess put an image on the big screen. It was a close-up of the PALS terms and conditions. It focused on these words:

PALS:
PUPIL AUTOMATED LOBOTOMY SCHEME

Certain words have an OP effect: you only have to say them and you can whip people into an angry frenzy. With teachers, it's 'Ofsted'; with *Star Wars* fans, it's 'Jar Jar Binks'; for a bunch of parents who had just handed their kids over to an evil maniac, without reading the terms and conditions, it was 'Pupil Automated Lobotomy Scheme'. Everyone was shouting and jumping out of their seats.

But we had one last card to play.

'Hey! Everyone! I have one more thing to show you before you take Miss Smilie down to Chinatown.'

The noise died down. People actually wanted to hear what I had to say and I'm not going to lie, it made me feel Tony Stark powerful.

'With a bit of help from a friend, my sidekick and I have discovered that the lobotomy sparking procedure has some side effects. I could describe them to you, but it's better if you see them for yourselves. Here's what happens to a PAL if they see or hear something that goes against Miss Smilie's teachings.'

I nodded at Jess and she clicked 'play' on the clip we'd been working on. It used the same images as the PALS ones, but we'd replaced disapproving Simon with smiling Simon. Jess had chosen the music to go with it. It was something called 'Anarchy in the UK' by an old band my dad liked. As she turned up the volume until the hall shook, what we hoped would happen started to happen.

First the PALS went pale. Then they started to sway in their seats and scrape at their faces with their fingernails. Some of them cried; some of them screamed; some of them pulled out their own hair. Lots of them grabbed their stomachs. Then they turned green and began to retch and convulse, just a little bit at first but then really wildly. And then they puked. Loads and loads of puke. Lumpy, stinky puke. All over themselves, the floor, their parents.

As everybody in the hall went nuts, I looked over to where Miss Smilie stood at the back of the hall, surrounded by pigeons and covered in poo and feathers. Her hair was a mess and her lipstick was smeared across her face. She wasn't smiling anymore. For a second our eyes met, then she turned and made a run for it.

'Stop her!' Jess shouted, as Smilie reached the double doors.

And that was when I had another one of my awesome ideas. 'Hey, PALS,' I tried to whistle, forgetting that I'm a really bad whistler. 'HEY, PALS!' I yelled as loudly as I could to be heard over the chaos. I had to hand it to Smilie, she'd done such a good job of training the PALS that even after wildly puking and being pulled into corners by their horrified parents, hundreds of pale faces turned my way. They just had to follow instructions.

'Your good friend, Miss Smilie,' I said as Smilie turned and looked at me over her shoulder, 'is feeling very sad and very glum...'

'We must hug our chum!' the PALS said and ran towards her, arms outstretched. Miss Smilie disappeared under a pile of sick-covered children, screaming and yelling, 'Get off me you stupid, mindless brats!'

Mission accomplished.

I looked at Jess and saluted.

She rolled her eyes and mouthed back at me, 'Idiot.'

20

The Aftermath

Me and Jess had to give statements to the police. We'd decided that we would tell them the things they needed to know to put Miss Smilie in prison, but keep some stuff secret. We explained about sparking to freeze people's brains and about the subliminal messages. We even told them the muffin analogy. But we didn't say that it was possible to use the procedure in the opposite way. We didn't tell them about our powers.

Imagine what would happen if the world found

out there was a way to get superpowers. Some people would do anything to be able to detect lies, or communicate with animals, or any of the other abilities that Miss Fortress knew how to spark into life. If The Professor's knowledge fell into the wrong hands it would be bad, bad times for everyone.

So we told a few lies. Because sometimes, not very often and only for the very best reasons, a lie can be a good thing.

We tried to tell the police about Montgomery McMonaghan and SPARC, but they said there was no evidence to prove Miss Smilie was following his orders. Miss Fortress thinks McMonaghan has moles (not actual giant mutant moles – that would be stupid, apparently – moles are like dirty cops) helping him in the police force. It was pretty scary to think about him getting away with his evil schemes and being untouchable.

The next morning, Miss Fortress had the job of changing all the blueberries back, starting with our friend.

As I walked to the Friendship Bench at first break, I heard a giggle behind me and felt a sharp shove in my back. Normally I'd be annoyed, but it was good to know that things were getting back to normal. Jess and Darth Daver were sitting on the bench, laughing, as Pushatron ran off. Dave didn't look quite his old self, because while Miss Fortress can apparently do a lot of cool things, she cannot 'magically grow back hair'. Jess looked a bit different too. She looked happy.

'Darth Daver and Jessticles, sitting in a tree, K.I.S.S ... I mean ... discussing which outfits they want to be buried in when they die.'

'Shut up, stink-boy.'

'Just telling it like it is, Jessticles, no need for the abuse.'

'So have you decided yet?'

Miss Fortress had offered to take my power away. Apparently it would involve another spark and a short, sharp pain, and then I'd be rid of it for good. She was even 89.4 percent sure she could do it without leaving me with any permanent brain damage.

I'd thought about it for a minute or two. There was a time when I'd have done almost anything to ditch the lie detector and get back to my old life. But things had changed. I had better control of it now, so I only stunk about half the time. I'd also got pretty good at using it to find out what I wanted to know; other secret agents would kill to have that kind of power. And most of all, if I changed back to normo-Alex, I'd miss working with Jess. It had been the most fun time of my life.

'Yep, I'm keeping it. Miss Fortress has a worrying lack of concern for child welfare. If I let her near me with another electric shock, I'll probably end up with an even worse side effect, like a really annoying laugh, or not being able to eat sausages anymore.'

Jess smiled and nudged me in the ribs with her bony elbow. 'I'm glad,' she said.

I smiled back.

'Besides, it's only a matter of time until Agent Alex and The Ballbruiser have another case to crack. Emerging from the debris of their battle with the Lobotomiser comes a new foe for the heroic squad to defeat. Bigger. Badder. Less lipsticky...'

Jess didn't even bother telling me to stop, she just sighed. Dave laughed and squeezed her hand.

'Come on, Ballbruiser,' I said, 'you can hum our theme tune in the background while I narrate.'

'No.'

'What song did you settle on for the theme tune?' Darth Daver asked.

'Don't encourage him, Dave!'

'Just ignore Jessticles,' I said, 'I always do. Anyway, I'm still deciding between a few. I could use your help, actually. Ooh, and I need to think of a codename for you. How about Cybershadow?'

After Bob's heroic act of self-sacrifice in the PALS suite, me and Jess had assumed he was lost. I knew from my previous, erm, experiment that too much Red Bull could be lethal to a goldfish. That and him being out of water for so long should have killed him. And if that hadn't, being down Smilie's top would have finished anyone off. But Bob was no ordinary fish.

After we escaped, Dexter and one of his associates managed to pick Bob up and drop him in the PALS aquarium. He was badly bruised and we had to keep him in a dark room for a few days while the effects of the Red Bull wore off, but Bob was a tough little dude and eventually he made a full recovery.

Jess and me wanted to do something to say

thanks, so we brought him a very special present. We got back from school and placed a jar next to his tank. Inside it was a white and orange fish, with large, ruffled fins and amber eyes.

'Bob,' Jess said, 'you remember Elle.'

Bob stopped swimming his circuits and stared, which I guess was his version of being speechless.

'She's come to live with us,' I said. I uncovered a tank, more colourful and with more stuff in it than Bob's, and gently tipped Elle into her new home. Jess and I slid the tank across the breakfast bar so they were next to each other.

'We thought you guys should have your own space, until you get to know each other better.' One step at a time, after all.

'What do you think?' Jess asked; but instead of answering, Bob did a back flip.

'I think he's happy,' I said. 'And more importantly we might be able to get out of Friday night Scrabble now. You've got to be pretty messed up if you have to resort to blackmailing people into playing word games with you.'

'Alex!'

'Come on, Jess. I love the little dude but we both know he has some issues.'

'Oh. My. God!'

'I don't mean it in a horrible way – it's just he needs to loosen up a bit.'

'Alex! HE CAN HEAR YOU!'

Oops. Bob, Elle and Jess just stared at me with the same expression on their faces, which I wouldn't have thought was possible considering two of them were fish.

'Sorry, Bob.'

Jess rolled her eyes. 'Have you learnt nothing over the past few weeks?'

I thought about how much things had changed since that pop-up appeared on my computer. I'd gained a power and a stink which led to me losing my super-cool reputation and the people who I thought were my friends. But when I found myself at the bottom of the deepest, darkest, loneliest hole I could ever have imagined, it gave me the chance to stop and look around me. What did I see? I saw unexpected people willing to help me climb out. I saw Jess: ferocious, honest and loyal. I saw Darth Daver – Dave: kind, compassionate and clever. I saw Bob: strange, sly and determined. Most of all I saw me, Alex Sparrow: smart, brave and a little bit weird. We all have things about us that are awesome, and other things that we don't like so much – things that make us feel like we don't fit in. We are all unique, every single one of us, and there's nothing wrong with that. In fact, I preferred my new friends and my new life. And I liked the new Alex much better than the old Alex. I wasn't about to tell Jess that though.

I smiled. 'Nope, nothing, Jessticles. Nothing at all.'

Alex and Jess face an unexpected enemy and a
whole host of animals with attitude
in their next adventure:

ALEX SPARROW AND
THE FURRY FURY

About the Author

Jennifer Killick always wanted to be a writer, but really started when she applied for a Creative Writing MA at Brunel University, which is where she first got the idea for Alex Sparrow. She lives in London, in a house full of children, animals and Lego. When she isn't busy mothering or step-mothering (which isn't often) she loves to read, write and run, as fast as she can. Jennifer's favourite things are books, trees and fluffy slippers, and her favourite place in the world is her home, where she can sit in her pyjamas with tea and cake, coming up with story ideas.

www.jenniferkillick.com

Acknowledgements

I feel like the luckiest girl in the world to be writing the acknowledgements for my very own novel. But that's the thing – this novel isn't just mine – it belongs to all of the people who helped me along the way.

I was lost when I met Imogen Cooper. Not only did she guide me through turning my manuscript from a muddle into a publishable story; she filled me with confidence and helped me to fall in love with writing again. For that I will always be grateful.

I would also like to thank my brilliant agent, Kirsty McLachlan. From the moment I met her, I knew I wouldn't find a better person to hand my story to.

Enormous thanks to the team at Firefly: Penny Thomas, Janet Thomas and Meg Farr. I can't imagine a lovelier group of people to work with – passionate, committed and kind. I'm so proud to be a Firefly.

I am in love with my awesome cover. Thank you, Alex Dimond, for your perfect design and thank you, Heath McKenzie, for your brilliant illustrations.

Thanks, also, to Jane Carter at Waterstones, Sarah Penny at Brunel University, and to Jo Clarke and MG Leonard. Your support means so much.

I have been extremely fortunate to have made some amazing friends while on my writing journey. Vashti Hardy: you inspire me every day with your unwavering kindness and your incredible talent. And Lorraine Gregory: you help me to laugh through the anxiety, and you have the answers to all questions. I don't know what I'd do without you both.

To my friends at The Golden Egg Academy, especially Kay Vallely, James Nicol, Lisa Sorrell, Rus Madon, Anthony Burt, Andrew Wright and Alex Campbell: you showed me that you should never underestimate the importance of a kind word at the right moment. I'm grateful to every Egg who has offered me their support. You are a generous and talented bunch.

Thank you to my oldest friends: Laura Endersby, Nicola Wareing, Emma Savin and Sarah Hill, for all the years of support and love and for always being on my side.

Thanks to my mum, Trish, my dad, Dave and my sister, Julie, for never telling me I was stupid to try, and for helping in so many ways. And to Alfie, who is never afraid to say what he thinks. I look forward to hearing your review of The Stink… Thanks, also, to the aunts, uncles and cousins who have been cheering me on.

To Stanley: this book is full of you. Without you, Alex Sparrow would probably never have existed, or if he did, he'd be very different. You fill my life with sunshine, swag dance moves and laughter. And to Teddy: having you proved to me that dreams can come true if we refuse to give up. You are a delight and watching you grow every day is such a joy.

My stepchildren swept into my life midway through writing The Stink, and have made a huge impact. To Mia, who is brave and kind and one of my favourite people to be around; to Helena, the clever little dreamer who so often reminds me of myself; and to Luis, who is sweet and spirited and makes me laugh so hard I cry: thank you all so much.

And finally, to Dean, who took on more than he should so that I could be free to dream-chase. I couldn't have done this without you.